To Joyce

Best wishes from

Sue.

# The Call of the Peacock

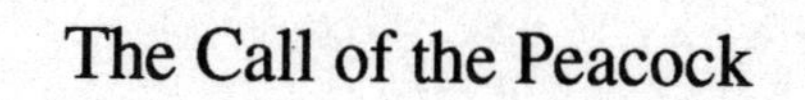

*By the same author*

Fortune's Bride

# The Call of the Peacock

SUSAN UDY

ROBERT HALE • LONDON

First published in Great Britain 1994

ISBN 0 7090 5488 2

Robert Hale Limited
Clerkenwell House
Clerkenwell Green
London EC1R 0HT



Printed and bound by Interprint Limited,
Valletta, Malta.

# One

Kathy stared at Bill, the *Chronicle*'s editor and her boss, not knowing precisely what response to make. She felt sickened and shocked by what he'd just told her and even more shocked by what he was asking her to do.

'There's another story there somewhere; I know it. You'll be perfect – coming in with a fresh eye, so to speak. As you were in Bosnia six months ago when it happened you know nothing about the case therefore you won't have any preconceptions about it.'

'But I'm supposed to be the paper's foreign affairs correspondent, Bill, not. . . .'

'Aw, come on, love, you were always so good at this sort of thing. Nobody else gets at the truth like you do. I never should have agreed to you taking over as foreign correspondent,' Bill went on to grumble. 'The new chap's just not up to investigative work. Please, just this once. Then you can revert to the overseas stuff, I promise.'

'But, surely, as I wasn't here at the time of her suicide I won't have the foggiest idea about the circumstances surrounding it. It will all have gone a bit cold by now, won't it? And it does seem insensitive – to say the least – to resurrect something that her family and friends will surely wish to forget. . . .'

'No, no.' Bill waved her objections aside. 'People will view it in a different light now. Have a better perspective on things just because it's over and done with; they won't object to talking about it. You get down there, Kathy, dig around a bit, ask questions. You know the sort of thing. Good grief, girl, you've done it dozens of times before. It'll make a change for you after Bosnia. You know what I want. Why did the wife of a well-known and extremely rich writer kill herself when, on the face of it, she had everything to live for? One child already; another on the way. Here,' – Bill thrust a bundle of newspapers at her – 'there are all the reports and stories that were published at the time. Familiarize yourself with them. They implied that there was more to it then but no one could find anything concrete. The local residents all clammed up. Richardson is quite a hero in those parts by all accounts and they stood by him to a man – and a woman. Nobody would say a word about it all.' He smiled brightly up at her. 'If anyone can find out the truth, you can. Don't let me down. We need a scoop to increase our circulation. It's been steadily dropping and the powers that be are starting to get fidgety.'

Kathy made herself a cup of coffee later that evening at her flat and sat down, preparing herself for the task of reading each of the reports that Bill had handed her.

Esther Richardson.

She stared down at the photograph that graced the front page of the first of the newspapers that her editor had given her. There was one thing that Kathy hadn't told Bill while he had been urging her to look into Esther's suicide. She knew Esther – had known Esther, rather. They'd lived next door to each other for fifteen years and their ways had only parted when Esther had met Jake and been swept off her feet and straight into marriage with him at the age of nineteen. Esther had then gone to live in Cornwall and Kathy had stayed in London, finding herself a job on the *Chronicle* – where she'd been ever since. That had been ten years ago and Kathy had done well in that time, moving up from the position of junior and then investigative journalist to foreign affairs correspondent, which explained her presence in Bosnia at the time of Esther's suicide. She'd been sent there to report back on a weekly basis on the conditions in Sarajevo's orphanages. It had been harrowing work and she'd been heartily relieved when she was suddenly and unexpectedly summoned back to England. That was until she'd heard of Esther's death today.

Kathy looked now at the newspaper photo of Esther. It wasn't the face of a woman contemplating suicide and yet, according to the report, it had been a recent picture of her. Esther was smiling and looked more or less as Kathy remembered her. Alongside the photo of Esther was another photograph. It had clearly been taken with a telephoto lens because it was slightly blurred. But it was recognizably Jake Richardson. The only way that Kathy knew this – apart from the man's name printed beneath the picture – was because Esther had sent her one of the wedding photos. Jake was leaving the house and striding towards his car. A third picture showed a small girl. This must be Lucy.

Kathy began to read the reports of Esther's death, but first, she glanced back at the photo of Esther. Why would Esther do such a thing? She searched her former friend's features for any signs of distress, of desperation. There were none. But the photograph had been taken a month before her death and as Kathy had discovered, time and time again in the course of her work as a journalist – a lot could happen in a month.

It appeared that Esther's body had been found by a chambermaid in one of the bedrooms of a local hotel when she went to clean the room the next morning. The doctor had confirmed that Esther had been dead for some hours. Why go to a hotel? But then again, why not? Kathy reasoned. It was as good a place as any. And presumably it would ensure that she wasn't found before the pills had done their work.

Jake, when interviewed, had denied all knowledge of why his wife should be in the hotel. 'I was in London overnight – as I told the police. I was informed upon my return the next morning of my wife's death by Sergeant Toms.'

'But what was she doing at The Smuggler's Arms?' the reporter had asked. 'Why wasn't she at home? Had she gone to meet someone?'

But Jake Richardson had refused to be drawn. In fact, if the reporter was to be believed, he'd all but thrown the man bodily from his house.

The next paper that Kathy picked up confirmed that Jake Richardson had indeed been in London on the night of his wife's death but with his daughter and her 'glamorous' nanny – and that was the report's exact terminology.

*When questioned as to what he was doing in London with an attractive woman who wasn't his wife Mr Richardson curtly told us that he was on 'private and personal' business which was nothing to do with anyone else'.*

*Sergeant Toms had nothing to add to this*, the paper diligently went on. And then proceeded, along with several other of the more unsavoury newspapers, to offer their dubious evidence and finally conclude that Jake Richardson had, with his clear infidelity with his daughter's nurse, driven his wife to take her own life. But, nonetheless, despite their industrious guesswork and prolonged harassment of anyone known to be concerned with the affair, no one could come up with anything concrete to bear out this theory. At the end of the day, they'd had to admit it was all down to nothing more substantial than speculation and surmise. When the papers finally abandoned their trial by media of Jake, no one was any the wiser about the real reasons for Esther Richardson's dramatic suicide. One paper had even gone so far as to print a photograph of Lucy's nurse, Pauline Duvall, and Kathy had to admit that she was a beautiful woman.

Kathy remained thoughtful as she heaped the papers back together. Had the papers in their mad quest for the truth, in fact, got it right? Had Esther discovered that Jake and Pauline Duvall were having an affair and thus, knowing she was pregnant with Jake's second child, felt desperate enough to kill herself? Or had Jake perhaps threatened to leave her for Pauline Duvall and Esther, in a bid to morally blackmail him into staying with her, attempted a suicide bid that had gone tragically wrong? But, in that case, Kathy concluded, she wouldn't have chosen a hotel bedroom with no possible chance of being found in time. Kathy made one of her lightning decisions. For the sake of their past friendship, she owed it to Esther to find out – to put the record straight if she possibly could. Her friend couldn't possibly have anticipated the torrent of suspicion and speculation that her unexpected death would unleash. Kathy would do as Bill wanted and go to Cornwall. But not simply to dig for a story for publication. She'd work flat out to find the truth behind the suicide and when she did – if she did, she silently amended – then, and only then, would she decide what to write or not write. If she felt the truth wasn't sufficiently palatable for publication then she'd tell Bill that there was nothing to report – other than what had already been said – in plenty. The curious thing about all of this, she felt, was that Esther hadn't left a note. The omission didn't match up with what Kathy remembered of her friend. Esther had always been a gregarious person and the Esther of their youth would have certainly wanted everyone to know her reasons for such a final step. If someone had indeed driven her to commit suicide, then the Esther that Kathy had known ten years ago would have wanted the world to know precisely who it was in the driving seat. Esther's silence was out of character. Bill was right; there was something more to this than there appeared on the surface.

And who knows, perhaps he would be proved right about people's willingness to talk – six months later. As he had said, 'You know what these small villages can be like, hotbeds of gossip. And Cornwall's no different to anywhere else, you can take it from me. I should know. I've spent enough holidays down there.'

The next morning Kathy was in the process of throwing sufficient clothes into a suitcase for a stay of a week or possibly two when her doorbell rang.

It was David, the current man in Kathy's life.

'I'm glad you've come, David,' she said, 'it saves me a phone call.'

David glanced down at the case. 'You aren't being sent off somewhere else, surely? You've only just got back.'

'Cornwall, I'm afraid.'

'Cornwall! Whatever for?'

'Bill wants me to go and investigate a suicide.'

'Oh? Whose?'

'Do you remember something that happened six months ago? The suicide of Esther Richardson?'

'The writer's wife? Yes. Why?'

'That's where I'm going. Bill senses a story – more of a story than was uncovered at the time. And after reading the reports on it, I'm rather inclined to agree with him. . . .'

'So, he's sending you to do his dirty work for him, is he? Bit of a come-down, isn't it? After the glories of Bosnia and its starving orphans. . . .'

'I consider that a rather unfortunate choice of words, David,' Kathy heatedly chastised, 'if you could have seen the plight of those children at first hand you wouldn't be quite so glib. . . .'

'Sorry. You're right, of course. It's simply that you've only just got back, darling, and I was hoping we'd see something of each other.'

'I know, David, but it is my job.' She paused then, wondering how much she should tell David until, swamped by a feeling of disloyalty to him, she hastened on, 'But that's not my main reason for going.'

'Oh? What is then?' He was eyeing her curiously now.

'Do you recall me telling you – some time ago now – about my closest friend during my schooldays and for a while beyond?'

'Which one in particular? You've talked about several.'

'The one who got married and went to Cornwall. . . . ?'

'Oh, that one.' He glanced sharply at her. 'You don't mean. . . .'

'Yes, I do actually. It was Esther.'

'Good Lord. And you've just found out presumably. But you haven't seen anything of her for years, have you? Why do you need to rush off. . . .?'

'Just over five years actually. The last time was just before her little girl was born. Bill feels that something's not right about it all and, upon reflection, I agree with him. If Esther had been driven to kill herself – she would have wanted the world to know why. But she left no note. The coroner concluded that the balance of her mind was disturbed – in other words, she was mad. I don't believe it. Look at her photograph.' Kathy thrust the newspaper at him. 'Does that look like a woman who was disturbed enough to take her own life and that of her unborn child? That was taken a month before her death. What happened to her in that last month to precipitate her into such an extreme course of action?

There's something wrong about it all, David. Something that someone wasn't telling.'

'Someone?' David echoed.

'Yes, someone knew more at the time than they were letting on.'

'You mean the husband? Jake Richardson?'

Kathy shrugged. 'Possibly. But that's what I mean to find out.'

'You're not going to get yourself too involved, are you, Kathy? Only I know what you're like when you get your teeth into something.' David regarded her doubtfully. 'I mean, it's not as if you and Esther were still close . . . You only visited her once or twice after she married, didn't you?'

'My work made it difficult. Our main point of contact was our letters and even those stopped about three-four years ago.'

'You must know her husband then?'

'No, I don't. The papers suggested that he was being unfaithful to Esther with Lucy's nurse. . . .'

'Yes, I remember. But there was absolutely no evidence of that.'

'No, I know, and yet, I have this gut feeling about it. Anyway, for my own peace of mind, I intend going there and seeing what I can dig up.'

'Where is it that you're going?'

'Trezillian. Esther and Jake lived in a big, old house just outside the village. Peacock House.'

'How come you never met Richardson?'

'They met and married all within a month – while I was in France on holiday. No,' she laughed, when she saw his expression, 'nothing like that. Jake Richardson played the gentleman right up until their wedding night

– at least, that's what Esther said. There was no question of it being a rushed marriage for any other reason than love at first sight. Jake fell like a ton of bricks, apparently, and saw no reason to wait to make Esther his bride. He was twelve years older than her. They'd left on their honeymoon by the time I got back, from which they returned directly to the house in Trezillian.'

'Impatient, wasn't he? He must have formidable powers of persuasion that's all I can say,' David grumbled. 'Here's me,' he went on, 'been badgering you to marry me now for two years and still the answer's no.' Although David's tone was light, Kathy knew, from his initial tone, how deeply he'd been hurt by her repeated refusals to marry him.

'I'm sorry, David, I really am.'

'You're sorry,' he sighed. 'That makes two of us.'

'David. . . .' Kathy began.

'Don't say you're sorry again,' he retorted, 'I really couldn't stomach it. I have to go.' He put his arms around her, pulling her into him, kissing her with a passion he didn't normally demonstrate. David was a man who kept his emotions very much to himself. Perhaps that was why he seemed unable to inspire love in her.

But the truth was that Kathy didn't really know what she felt for David. Oh, she was fond of him, very fond. They'd been going out together now for three years. But somehow, their kisses lacked that intensity, that urgency that Kathy wanted to feel before she would agree to marry anyone. There was no rush of the heated desire that she'd read about and written about, moreover, in her novels. The love scenes that she described so faithfully in her books were mere products of her imagination. She smiled bitterly to herself. It was a wonder that her readers didn't discern that.

Once David had gone, she sat, nursing an empty coffee cup. Why couldn't she love him? Why hadn't she been able to love any man? Why couldn't she physically respond to him as he so obviously wanted her to. At twenty-nine she should be married with children. All her friends were. She smiled wryly. Yet, here she was, still with nothing more significant in her life than her writing and her job with the local newspaper.

She stood up and went into the kitchen to rinse out her cup before she set off for Trezillian. There must be something wrong with her, she mused, as she had done a million times before. But whatever the reason for her coldness, she knew she wasn't being fair to David. She should make a decision, one way or the other. Either marry him, as he wanted, or let him go. . . .

# Two

When she got to Trezillian, Kathy checked into the only hotel that the small town seemed to possess, The Smuggler's Arms; the same hotel that Esther's body had been discovered in six months ago. As she always did, she gave the name that she used for her journalistic work, Jennifer Bell. Jennifer was Kathy's middle name and she'd begun to use it in conjunction with the abbreviated form of her surname, Bellamy, believing that it would disassociate her from her other line of work, that of romantic novelist. She'd suspected that if people knew she also wrote what she described as 'silly romances', they wouldn't take the investigatory work that she did for the *Chronicle* seriously. And it had to be said, her novel writing had never earned enough money to live on so her work for the paper was a necessity rather than a calling. It also regularly provided her with usable plots for her books.

''Ere on 'oliday, are you?' the porter asked as he hefted her case up the stairs. The Smuggler's Arms didn't run to the luxury of a lift.

'No. I'm here to look into a death.'

'Oh?' the porter now said, shooting her an overtly enquiring glance. 'Whose death would that be then? Not still Esther Richardson's, surely? That 'appened five-six months ago now.'

'Yes, I know. But my editor wants a follow-up story. You know,' she went on chattily, 'how the family are coping, that sort of thing . . . .'

'Oh, I see. You'm one of them reporters. Gawd, we had dozens of them blighters 'ere at the time. Like terriers they wuz. They must 'ave said all there was to say then I'd 'ave thought. Can't be much left. Bit macabre, ain't it? A follow-up? Like one of them there films. You know, the sequel to . . . and all that.'

As that had been Kathy's sentiments exactly at the time of Bill's request, she stayed silent, simply shrugging at the man. Then, 'It's orders. And it's what my editor wants. Who am I to argue? It's a job. . . .'

'What paper you from then?'

'The *Chronicle*.'

'Never 'eard of it.'

'No, you wouldn't have. It's a London paper.'

'Oh, I see.'

'Which room was she found in?' That was one fact that the papers hadn't given at the time.

'Room twenty two. The chambermaid found 'er when she went in to clean.'

'It seems strange – her coming here to do it,' Kathy guilelessly remarked. 'Any ideas why she should do that? You must have known her after all. You being a local man. . . .'

The man smiled self-importantly. 'Well, I do 'ave my own theories about that but I don't usually. . . .' He paused then, eyeing her sideways, as if trying to decide whether she was a worthy recipient of whatever snippet of information he was about to impart. 'She'd been 'ere – to the bar – more than once for a drink – always alone. . . .'

'Davis.' A tall, thin man came towards them. 'You're wanted in reception. Take the lady to her room and come down straight away.'

'Yes, sir. Right away, sir. 'Ere you are, miss. Room twenty-eight.

'Sorry, miss. I've 'ad strict instructions not to talk to anyone – well, we all 'ave, all the staff – 'specially not to newspaper reporters. The manager's a bit touchy about it 'appening here and no-one finding her till mornin'. And like you, miss, I 'ave to do as I'm told or else risk losing my job. . . .'

Later, when Kathy was unpacking her bag in her room, she wondered anew about what the porter had said about Esther. 'She'd been here – to the bar – more than once for a drink – always alone.' She didn't recall that fact being mentioned in the newspaper reports. Perhaps neither they nor the police had considered it important enough to mention. And maybe it wasn't. But to drink alone? When Kathy had known her, Esther had been an intensely social person, loving people around her; almost needing people around her. So why would Esther come here – alone – for a drink? And why that evening? Her husband was going to be away with the nanny and Lucy. Esther must have known that. And although Esther and Jake employed a housekeeper, the papers had said that the woman had been out for the evening. Esther would have known that she would be returning later. Perhaps she had been frightened that the woman would find her too soon? But surely a mere housekeeper wouldn't take it upon herself to check her employer's bedroom before retiring for the night? Unless they'd reason to believe that Esther might be thinking of taking her own life and she knew that her husband had asked the housekeeper to keep an eye on her? Was that it? Had Esther tried to end it all before? Another possibility presented itself to Kathy then, one that sent a chill right through her. Had Jake, knowing that, and wanting his freedom without the messy business of a very public divorce, deliberately gone to London with his mistress, leaving his wife alone, in the hope that she'd try again to kill herself and this time, succeed?

'Come and sit down, Miss Bell,' the round-faced sergeant invited as he turned to a large filing cabinet and pulled out a manilla document holder. 'Just the details of Mrs Richardson's case. Now, tell me, how can I help you? Although it's a bit late in the day. The case has been closed for quite some time.'

'Yes, I know. But my paper wants to do a follow-up on it. How the family have coped since, that sort of thing. As I read it, Mrs Richardson took an overdose of sleeping pills?'

'Yes – along with an entire bottle of red wine. She meant to kill herself all right.' The last was said with a certain amount of self-satisfaction.

'Was there ever any doubt about that?' Kathy asked lightly.

'Well, these things can sometimes be an accident when they happen at home. They take one dose of their usual sleeping pill, go to sleep, wake up and take another. . . .' He shrugged. 'But to come to an hotel and swallow a whole bottle full and then follow up with a bottle of red wine . . . well, in my book, that makes it quite deliberate. The coroner thought so too.'

'But she sometimes did go to the hotel, it appears.'

'Who's been telling you that?'

'The porter.'

'I see.'

'It wasn't made public at the time, was it? Mrs Richardson's liking for a lone drink?'

'No.'

'Why was that?'

'Mr Richardson asked us not to say anything.'

'Oh,' Kathy exclaimed sardonically, 'Mr Richardson asked you not to!'

'Yes.'

'Why should he do that?'

The sergeant shrugged. 'Didn't want his wife's name blackened, I suppose.'

'Why would that blacken Mrs Richardson's name?'

The man shrugged again. 'Well, you know, woman drinking alone in bar – all sorts of interpretations could be placed upon that.'

'Like what?'

'Well – that she liked the drink a bit too much. Was there to pick up a man.'

'And was she?'

'Was she what?'

'There to pick up a man?'

'Look, miss, I don't know what your real intentions

are in coming here and asking all these questions....'

'I've just told you, Sergeant,' Kathy smiled sweetly, the very picture of innocence, 'I'm here to do a follow-up....'

'Yes, yes. I know that's what you've said,' he looked suspiciously at her, 'but Mr Richardson is highly thought of in these parts, a much respected man. The case has been closed. It was very much open and shut. Mrs Richardson was discovered with an empty pill bottle as well as an empty wine bottle at her side. Her fingerprints were all over both of them. It was obvious. Suicide – while the balance of her mind was disturbed. Now, let's leave it like that, shall we? And leave Mr Richardson to get on with his life – undisturbed by further innuendo and muck-racking.'

Kathy felt irritated. The police sergeant seemed far more concerned with smoothing Jake Richardson's pathway and avoiding any unpleasantness for him than with the reasons behind Esther's untimely death.

'There was no one at Peacock House on the night that Mrs Richardson died,' Kathy briskly went on. She refused to be fobbed off so easily. 'So why go to The Smuggler's Arms to end her life? Why not simply do it at home, in her own bedroom?'

'Well . . . presumably she feared being found too soon – before the pills could have taken effect. . . .'

'But the house was empty all night – apart from the housekeeper, that is. Was it usual for the woman to look in upon Mrs Richardson?'

'No, of course not.' The sergeant looked as offended as if it were he having doubt cast upon his motives.

'Then why book into a hotel?'

'I don't know, Miss Bell.' The police sergeant was

showing signs of getting rattled. 'Who knows what a depressed person will do? And her own doctor confirmed that she'd been on tranquillisers for precisely that.'

'There was no suicide note.'

'No – but then they don't always leave a note. She was probably too intoxicated to write one anyway.'

'But wouldn't she have written it earlier? She obviously intended killing herself that night otherwise wh have the wine and the pills with her?'

'Who's to say? The poor woman was clearly not in her right mind.'

Kathy ignored that, going on to bluntly ask, 'Did anyone see her carry the bottle of wine into the hotel?

'No.'

'Did she purchase it there perhaps?

'Apparently not.'

'Then where did she get it from?'

'Well, obviously she took it with her, Miss Bell.' The sergeant bestowed a decidedly superior smile upon her. 'The handbag she was carrying and that was found in the room with her would easily have held it. It was one of those large pouch ones.'

'Was it a wine bottle with a cork?'

'No, screw top. It wasn't an expensive wine . . . .'

'I see. Did Mr Richardson admit to having an affair with his child's nurse?'

'No. Why should he if there'd been nothing going on?'

'Did you ask him, Sergeant?'

'No.' The man was looking distinctly uncomfortable by this time.

In fact, Kathy couldn't understand why he was allowing her to go on interrogating him in this fashion. Unless – unless he was trying to curb any suspicion upon her part that things weren't quite as straightforward as he insisted they were?

'Why didn't you ask him? All the newspapers were asking that question. I mean – for heaven's sake, the man was in London, overnight, with her and even you, Sergeant, can't deny that Pauline Duvall is a remarkably lovely woman.'

'I didn't ask him because I didn't consider it then, and I don't consider it now, any of our business. Now, Miss Bell, if you will excuse me, I do have work to do . . . .'

'What precisely did Mrs Richardson's doctor say about her state of mind, Sergeant?'

'That she'd been having trouble sleeping and seemed to be suffering from a high degree of anxiety. However, she'd refused to tell him what was the cause of this so he'd prescribed Mogadon – three weeks supply. Which' – he glanced down at his notes at this point – 'which she would have run out of a week or so before her suicide, the doctor said. He had refused to renew the prescription, fearing dependency, so. . . .'

'She'd run out! So how did she overdose herself, Sergeant?'

'The container found at the scene of her death had contained Sodium Amytal.'

'Which is?'

'A barbiturate.'

'Why would she have been taking those?'

'Well, the theory was that if her doctor had refused to prescribe more of the tranquiliser she had been taking – and he did say it would be fairly difficult to overdose on it in any case, you would need to consume large quantities – then she must have been determined enough to get hold of something else. In this case, Sodium Amytal. It's freely available on the black market, sadly. The combination of an overdose of that – added to whatever traces there were still in her body of the Mogadon – plus the wine would be pretty lethal. As I said, it was pretty much an open-and-shut case, I'm afraid, Miss Bell. Definitely suicide.'

# Three

Not all of what the police sergeant had told Kathy about Esther's suicide had appeared in the papers. The journalists in question had clearly been uninterested in the mechanics of the suicide; they'd been more concerned with the whys than any wherefores. Namely, had Jake Richardson and his child's nurse been indulging in a passionate love affair thereby driving Esther, in a fit of despair, to kill herself?

After a very disturbed night, Kathy decided to make Peacock House her first port of call that morning. She wanted to meet Jake Richardson for herself. Find out what sort of a man he was.

All she knew of him at the moment was what Esther had told her all those years ago. That Jake was a passionate, determined man; accustomed to having his way in all things. Very much the stronger partner of the marriage, she had suspected at the time – but that had been no surprise to Kathy. Esther, probably due to her intense love of life, could show herself to be amazingly irresponsible on occasion, living each moment for itself and hang the consequences, which made it all the more incredible that she would have, of her own volition, swallowed a lethal overdose.

Kathy withdrew a photograph from her handbag. Surprisingly, she'd always kept it by her. It was one of Esther and Jake, the only one she had of them together, and it had been taken on their wedding day.

Jake had been an astonishingly handsome man then. Kathy wondered if he still was or would age have softened the chiselled lines of jaw and brow, and blurred the astonishing clarity of the dark eyes? Would the odd grey strand have crept into the richly burnished, almost black hair? After all, he must be forty-one or two now. He was tall, six feet two or three, Kathy guessed, and powerfully built, with a long, well-shaped nose, and surprisingly, considering the rather harsh planes of his face, a full and sensuous mouth. That – sensuous look, allied with extreme wealth and his very evident self-possession, would make for a very powerful combination. Too powerful for many women to resist, Kathy decided. Hence the affair between Jake and Pauline Duvall?

Esther, standing alongside him, appeared delicate and feminine. Jake's arm was about her tiny waist, moulding her against his side, his bearing one of masterful possession. Esther's blonde head barely reached his shoulder. Sighing, Kathy stowed the photo away once more. That daintiness of Esther's had been the chief quality that Kathy had envied when they'd been growing up. Yet despite the doll-like appearance, Esther's body had been unmistakably that of a woman. Full breasts, curving waist and rounded hips, shapely legs and delicately boned ankles. Whereas, Kathy was tall for a woman, five feet seven, and her body, although perfectly proportioned was – almost boyish. 'Bean pole' they'd called her at school. Her breasts had never seemed to develop fully in her opinion, they'd remained small and high. She had a waist and hips to match, slender and gracefully curved; her legs were long, coltish almost. She sighed once more. No wonder everyone had compared her to a bean pole. She had no real curves to speak of – even now. She walked across to the full-length mirror and appraised her reflection. There was one feature that she did approve of, however – well, two actually. Her mane of rich chestnut hair and her large green eyes. She wouldn't exchange them for anything, not even for curves.

She ran down the hotel stairs and straight out into her car. She'd breakfasted earlier on fresh, locally caught mackerel and excellent coffee, so, at least, the inner woman was satisfied.

Curiosity rippled through her at the prospect of meeting Esther's husband.

The house when she approached it via a pair of high, wrought-iron, ornamental gates looked precisely the same as she remembered it from her occasional visit. Right down to the pair of stone peacocks – from which the house took its name – sitting in stately splendour on each side of the front door. Once upon a time, Esther had told her, the real thing had walked these lawns, their shrieking cries echoing through the tall trees. Now they could only be seen here, at the front entrance, and on the gates. A plaque on the centre of each featured the plumed head of the male bird.

Kathy climbed out of the car and approached the front door with uncharacteristic nervousness. She should have phoned first for an appointment. Jake might not even be here. For Jake Richardson wasn't only a prolific and highly successful writer; he was also the owner of a chain of extremely profitable and high-class supermarkets. It wasn't like her to be so careless.

However, she was in luck.

Her quick jabbing of the doorbell brought a plump. middle-aged woman to the door. The housekeeper, she guessed.

'Good morning. I wonder if I might see Mr Richardson.'

'Mr Richardson,' the woman looked doubtful. 'Well, I don't know. It's not really a good time . . . .'

'Who is it, Mrs Elliot?'

The richly timbred, slightly arrogant voice sounded from behind the woman and she swung, saying, 'It's a young woman asking to see you.'

'Well, who is it? Have you asked?' The tone betrayed impatience and Kathy once again felt the ripple of curiosity. The voice could only belong to one person: Jake.

'I'm from the *Chronicle* . . . .'

Before Kathy could finish, however, the owner of the voice strode to the door and Kathy found herself taking an instinctive step backwards, preparing herself for the sight of Esther's husband and whatever the consequences she might be provoking by turning up on his doorstep in such an impetuous manner.

Her precautions proved futile. Nothing could have prepared her for the sheer impact of the man himself.

Just as the photograph had indicated, he had been and still was an overwhelmingly handsome man. But the photograph had in no way revealed the charismatic quality of the flashing dark eyes, almost black as they raked her, or for the sheen of bronzed skin and the fullness of the mobile bottom lip.

'Yes,' he demanded. 'Who are you and what do you want?'

Kathy found herself swallowing convulsively, her throat suddenly dry beneath the scrutiny of those astonishing eyes.

She began to stammer, 'I'm – I'm . . . . K-Jennifer Bell . . . .' She'd almost introduced herself as Katherine. Had Jake noticed? She'd have to start thinking of herself as Jennifer, rather than Kathy. For on her way to Peacock House, Kathy had decided to keep her real identity a secret – even from Jake. It might inhibit him if he knew that she and his wife had once been close friends. People always seemed more inclined to talk to an impartial observer, she'd found, in the course of her investigative work. And she wanted to get Jake Richardson talking, freely and openly, about his relationship with Esther while she'd been alive.

'I'm from the . . . .' Her voice tailed off lamely. Did he have to contemplate her in quite such an arrogant manner? She tried again, more successfully this time. This man was having a most unusual effect upon her. It was an effect she didn't much care for. As a consequence, her voice hardened. 'I'm from the *Chronicle*. I'm here to do a feature – a follow-up feature, rather, on your wife. A sort of memorial . . . .'

'Oh God. Not another newspaper reporter!' he exclaimed in disgust. 'I should have thought that after all this time you people would have found some other story to get your avaricious teeth into. You're like vultures, aren't you? Hovering round the corpse, waiting for whatever morsel you can pick up.'

Jennifer blinked up at him. She could have thought of a more tasteful comparison than that one in the light of his wife's death; even if it had taken place six months ago.

'Oh, you'd better come in,' he invited wearily. 'Best to get it over with, I suppose. Perhaps then, finally, you blasted people will leave me alone? Bring a pot of coffee and two cups to the library, Mrs Elliot, would you?'

Jennifer, still not saying anything, followed the tall, lithe figure across the expanse of tiled hallway and through a door on the opposite side. The library, she saw, was a large room, with walls lined from floor to ceiling with bookshelves, of which two complete shelves carried copies of Jake Richardson's books. Jennifer had never read any of them, not caring for involved spy stories herself. But she knew people who raved about them. She'd heard that there were even negotiations going on to film a couple of them. Jake must have made a fortune out of his writing. It made her half a dozen novels that had been published look a bit sick. As yet, she hadn't made enough from them to do more than pay her monthly mortgage on her London flat. She grimaced ruefully. She noted the floor-length windows that led out to the garden and the two leather upholstered armchairs that flanked a huge, oak mantled fireplace. A long, polished refectory table sat in the middle of the room, upon which sat a shallow copper bowl of roses; they were giving out the most heavenly perfume. As it was July the garden was a riot of colour, glimpsed through the open window as Jennifer crossed the room towards the chair that Jake had indicated. Jennifer sat down and then wished she hadn't. For Jake elected to stand, one elbow propped casually upon the mantelpiece. She felt at a distinct disadvantage as Jake once again subjected her to a penetrating appraisal.

Jennifer wished he'd sit down as well. He seemed to tower over her, like some threatening monolith. To give herself something to do, she opened her handbag and pulled out her notepad and pen.

'Which paper did you say you'd come from?' The brisk, almost authoritarian tone startled her.

She glanced up to discover his dark gaze still fixed upon her.

'The *Chronicle*. It's a London paper so you probably won't have heard of it.'

'A London paper! What possible interest can you have in Esther after all this time? And why have you come all this way to talk to me about it?' He was contemplating Jennifer reflectively as he spoke. 'I would have thought there'd be more than enough material in the copies of all the newspapers at the time for your purposes. They certainly made a meal of it as I recall.' His tone was full of irony.

'Well, as I said, my editor is interested in doing a follow-up feature.'

'A follow-up feature!' Jake almost exploded. 'What's he expecting to hear? That I've married my daughter's nurse? Well,' he sneered contemptuously, 'it would make for a neat ending, I suppose. I'm only sorry that I have to disappoint you, Ms Bell.'

'I'm sure he wasn't expecting to hear that, Mr Richardson. After all, an item of such interest would surely have made all the national newspapers – in the light of the rumour and innuendo that were circulating at the time.' It was now Jennifer's turn to display irony.

'Was he one of the vultures who camped outside my door at the time of Esther's death?'

'I wouldn't think so, he doesn't normally go out on assignments himself.'

'No, he sends his minions to do his dirty work for him – someone like you.' Jake's glance was a strange one now as he openly weighed her up. There was clear hostility contained in it but there was something else as well. Something that Jennifer didn't recognize.

She felt herself stiffening, involuntarily. It was a great pity that Jake Richardson's personality didn't live up to the impression of charm that his looks so undoubtedly bestowed.

'I don't believe that there was anyone here from the *Chronicle* at the time. Bill – my editor, that is – felt that enough papers were covering it as it was – and we don't usually try to compete with the nationals. No, he's more interested in developments since.'

'There have been no developments – as you put it,' he continued harshly. 'Esther's dead – end of story.'

Jennifer felt herself flinching at his brutality. But she was determined not to be put off by his overt distaste for what she was doing here. 'I thought that perhaps you could tell me about your wife and the lead up to the . . . . ' Desperately, she searched for the right approach, anything to start him talking about Esther. Normally she didn't have this trouble. He was regarding her now with a slightly amused look. Jake Richardson was most certainly not fitting in with Jennifer's notions of a grieving husband. She knew it had all happened almost six months ago but even so . . . Her suspicions of him and his motives deepened.

'Esther would be flattered. What a pity she's not around to appreciate such interest,' he murmured drily.

Jennifer couldn't hide her shock at his manner.

'Oh dear, shocked you have I? Not quite what you expected?'

'Well, frankly, no,' Jennifer retorted, tightly.

He looked away from Jennifer then towards the door, where Mrs Elliot was bringing in the coffee.

'Thank you, Mrs Elliot. Put it down over there.' He indicated the low table to one side of Jennifer's chair. 'Perhaps you'd pour, Ms Bell?'

Jennifer, glad of something to occupy herself, poured the steaming black liquid into the delicate porcelain cups. This was turning out to be a very unusual interview. She wasn't quite sure how to continue.

To give herself time to think, she asked, 'Cream, sugar?'

'Neither, thanks.'

Once they both had cups in their hands, and with Jake, by this time, seated in the chair opposite to Jennifer, he glanced across at her and said, 'You don't resemble any of the newspaper reporters that I've encountered to date.'

'Really,' she responded with a cool smile. 'And what should I look like?'

'Oh,' he shrugged, 'slightly scruffy, studious . . . plain.'

Jennifer had never met anyone quite like Jake Richardson before. He had the power to disconcert so totally at his fingertips. She glanced up at him and was further disconcerted by the sudden flare of warmth within the dark eyes. Was this what had initially fascinated Esther? This – ability to surprise?

'Shocked you again, have I?' he drawled, almost insolently. 'You're very easily shocked for a woman in your profession.'

Jennifer cleared her throat and, putting her empty cup to one side, picked up her notepad again. She decided the easiest thing to do would be to completely ignore his last couple of remarks and simply get on with the interview. Sardonic amusement met her gaze when she lifted it to his face. Jake Richardson knew only too well the effect he had upon women. That was becoming increasingly clear. Well, he wasn't going to get to her.

'I believe you have just the one daughter?'

Jake crossed his one leg over the other and calmly met her gaze. 'Yes, Lucy.'

'And do you still employ the nurse, Pauline Duvall, to take care of her?' It was a daringly provocative question, she knew, in the light of his earlier remarks concerning the supposed relationship between himself and the woman. But it was a question that had to be asked.

Nonetheless, Jennifer couldn't suppress the tremor of apprehension that edged its way along her spine at the expression that appeared in Jake Richardson's dark eyes. All trace of the sardonic humour that she'd noted only moments ago had vanished. Now, his face was set in chiselled lines, rigorously shuttered against all scrutiny. 'Yes,' was all he said, however.

'How did your daughter take her mother's death? It must have had a pretty traumatic effect upon her.'

Jake put his cup down and abruptly got to his feet. 'I don't wish to discuss my daughter with you, Ms Bell.'

'Right,' Jennifer had long since learned to accept a

snub when one was administered during an interview. It was by far the best way. That didn't mean to say, of course, that she wouldn't return to the question when circumstances appeared more favourable. So that's what she did now, accepted Jake's rebuff and changed the subject. 'Had your wife given any indication that she was contemplating suicide? I believe it's not uncommon for jealous women, if they suspect that their husband is having an affair, to threaten suicide in order to bring the partner back into line?'

Jake didn't respond at all this time. Jennifer found herself holding her breath. It had been a sudden decision – to go for the hard line of questioning.

'I'd like you to leave, Ms Bell.'

Jake's tone was level but totally implacable, as was his gaze as it rested upon her. Jennifer conceded that she'd made a bad mistake. There'd be no shocking this man into saying anything he didn't want to. He was far too much in control of himself and his emotions.

'I'm sorry, that was clumsy of me.'

'Yes, it was. I don't respond to bludgeoning tactics. Now, if you don't mind, I have a lot to do.'

'Yes, of course.' Jennifer had always known when she was outclassed and she was well and truly outclassed this time. He'd never agree to another interview now – just when it was so important to find out all she could about the days – weeks leading up to Esther's suicide. She'd really messed it up. She stood up and held out a hand to him. 'I'm sorry if my questions offended you.'

Jake didn't respond to this overture. He also didn't take her hand. He simply turned away, saying, 'I'll show you out.'

So all Jennifer could do was follow him. Once she was standing outside the house again, she allowed her annoyance with herself to show. Damn. Damn. She'd handled him all wrong. But even so, the man was an arrogant chauvinist. Ordering her from the house like that. There'd been no pretence of grief at his wife's suicide. There'd also been no indication of guilt.

Jennifer was walking back to her car, still very much preoccupied with her thoughts, when the scrunching of gravel beneath small feet alerted her to the imminent arrival of someone else. A small girl ran round the side of the house, her blonde pigtails flying out behind her. She stopped at the sight of Jennifer.

'Who are you?' she demanded.

'Jennifer Bell.'

This was Lucy, Jennifer had no doubt of that. She was a miniature version of Esther. There were the same intensely blue eyes, the identical, almost white-blonde hair that Esther has possessed as a child, the same daintily made features and build. There wasn't a single thing that reminded Jennifer of the man she had just left – other than for the manner in which the child was regarding Jennifer. And that was Jake to a T. The haughty lift of the eyebrows, the scornful twist of the lips. Even at the age of five, Lucy possessed all the confident self-assurance of her father. She was unmistakably Jake and Esther's child. Jennifer smiled at her. 'And who are you?'

# Four

'I'm Lucy Richardson. What are you doing here?' the small child demanded. Her approach was every bit as forthright as her father's before her.

'I came to see your daddy.'

The girl studied Jennifer with interest. 'Why?'

'Well . . . I wanted to talk about your mummy.' Jennifer had been uncertain about mentioning Esther but this child seemed so . . . assured, so untouched by sorrow, that she decided to go ahead. And six months was a relatively long time in a child's calendar.

'My mummy's dead,' Lucy said with a bluntness that took Jennifer's breath clean away.

'Yes, I know,' murmured Jennifer. If she had considered Lucy Richardson a replica of Esther, she swiftly changed her mind. In all but appearance, she was most definitely her father's child. The same blunt candour; the same outspoken manner. No beating about the bush for this pair. Jennifer, as she had done with Jake only moments ago, searched for some indications of grief in this little girl. Shc found none. At least, none that were visible at first glance.

An immense pity for Esther took hold of her then. Did no one in this house mourn her?

'Have you seen Daddy?' Lucy went on to ask.

'Yes.'

'Did you know my mummy?' Lucy's gaze was direct and full of curiosity.

'A long time ago.' The words had slipped out. Jennifer bit her bottom lip in annoyance at her carelessness. Yet, this child seemed so honest, so open . . . it seemed a natural consequence to be equally as honest with her. Wrong, somehow, to tarnish her childish innocence with a lie.'

'Were you her friend?'

Jennifer hesitated again. How much should she tell Lucy? She decided to take a chance. 'Yes, once.

Lucy regarded her consideringly. 'When you were children? At school?'

'Yes.'

'Are you sad that she's dead?'

'Yes, I am, Lucy. You must be too.'

Lucy shrugged.

'Do you miss her?' Jennifer asked.

The small girl seemed to give careful consideration to the question. 'Sometimes,' she then said. 'Though – I didn't see her a lot.'

Jennifer studied the small, grave face. 'Why was that, Lucy?'

'Lucy! Where are you?' A woman's voice called from the rear of the house.

Lucy pulled a face. 'That's Pauline. She'll throw a tantrum if I don't go.'

Jennifer hid a smile. The child was old beyond her years. 'Is Pauline your nurse?' Although, of course, Jennifer knew she was.

'Yes.' Lucy turned to leave. 'Will you come again?'

'Do you want me to, Lucy?'

Lucy again gave the question some thought before answering. 'Yes. I think my mummy talked about you. But she didn't call you Jennifer. . . .'

Jennifer hastily interrupted. 'What did she say, Lucy?'

'That she missed you and would like to see you again. She wanted to talk to you . . . .'

'When did she say that, Lucy?'

But Lucy shrugged again. 'I can't 'member. Must go. Bye, Jennifer.' She began to run, then stopped. She swung to face Jennifer once more and asked for a second time, 'Will you come again?' From her expression, it was obvious to Jennifer that the child anticipated a refusal. What had made her so resigned to disappointment?

Not wanting to raise false hope in the little girl, Jennifer limited herself to a smiling, 'If I can, Lucy.'

'Why might you not be able to?'

'Your daddy might not want me to.'

'Oh.' The child's face fell. 'My daddy doesn't like me. Doesn't he like you either?'

Jennifer was conscious of shock again. Really, father and child were almost unnatural. An intense pity overwhelmed her – for a child who, in her own words, hadn't seen a lot of her mother and clearly believed her father only held her in dislike. She walked to Lucy and lowered herself until their faces were on a level.

'Lucy, I'm sure that's not so. Of course your daddy likes you.'

Lucy thrust her bottom lip out and shouted back, 'No, he doesn't. I heard him . . . .'

'Lucy! There you are.'

Lucy gasped and turned to face the owner of the voice. Jennifer straightened. Pauline Duvall was striding across the gravel towards them, her face set into frowning, irritable lines.

'Didn't you hear me calling you?'

Lucy glared back, rebellion evident in every stubborn line of her. 'Yes.'

'Then why didn't you come to me then?' Although she was addressing Lucy, the nurse's eyes were riveted upon Jennifer. 'Hasn't Daddy told you about talking to strangers?' The glacial gaze roved from Jennifer to her car. 'Can I help you?' The tone was as icy as the exceptionally lovely grey eyes.

True to the newspaper photograph, Pauline Duvall was a strikingly beautiful woman and not at all the type of person whom one would expect to discover in a position of child's nurse. No wonder Jake had taken her to London with him was Jennifer's first cynical thought. Her second was that it was no wonder that he was exhibiting no grief at his wife's unexpected death, not when he had this lovely creature to console him.

'This is Jennifer', Lucy put in. 'An old friend of Mummy's. You wouldn't know her, Pauline.' Lucy's tone was almost triumphant as she glanced up at her nurse. Did Lucy know what was going on between her father and this woman? If there was indeed something going on. Jennifer admitted that she didn't have any more proof of an affair between them than the papers had managed to glean at the time.

'I see.' Pauline's gaze was insolent now. 'Did you want to see her?'

Belatedly, Jennifer realized that she had made yet another mistake in telling Lucy that she had known Esther. For someone who was usually so adept at investigative assignments, she was making a real mess of this one. 'No,' Jennifer began to say before she was rudely interrupted by the other woman.

'Because she committed suic. . . .'

At Jennifer's sharp glance down at Lucy, who was all ears and eyes at the perceptible tension between her nurse and Jennifer, the woman did have the grace to bite back the words.

'I know,' Jennifer quietly said. 'That's why I've come. I'm a newspaper reporter so I'm here in my professional capacity, not as a friend. I've seen Mr Richardson.'

Pauline's glance slid over Jennifer now, assessing and appraising.

'You're a bit late, aren't you? It all happened nearly six months ago now.'

'Yes, I know.' Jennifer said no more. She had no intention of confiding the purpose behind her visit – or rather her ostensible purpose – to this insolent woman.

Undaunted by Jennifer's coolness, Pauline Duvall asked, 'Are you staying at the hotel?'

'Yes.'

'How long will you be staying for?'

'I really don't know at the moment.'

'I see.' Pauline Duvall paused, before saying, with undisguised rancour, 'Well, don't let us keep you.'

'Jennifer said she'd come and see me again – if she can.'

Pauline made no response to that and Jennifer, with a warmly reassuring smile at Lucy, turned and climbed into her car.

As Jennifer drove back to the hotel, the memory of Jake's shuttered expression when she had mentioned his daughter returned to her. Could it be that Lucy wasn't imagining her father's dislike as she had first supposed?

Jennifer was sitting in the the hotel's small lounge bar later that evening, reflecting upon what she'd found at Peacock House and what, if any, implications could be deduced from her findings, when she glanced up to see a beaming, ginger-haired man heading her way.

'What luck,' he retorted as he neared her. 'A new face and such an attractive one at that.' He held out a hand, 'Chris Williams. Local entrepreneur and importer of fine French wines and cheeses.' His brown eyes twinkled at her, conveying his admiration in no uncertain terms.

Jennifer smiled. A practised charmer if ever she saw one. But she admitted that it would be pleasant to have someone to talk to, and it would provide a welcome distraction from her anxieties over what had happened at Peacock House in the last weeks of Esther's life. There was also a strong possibility that Chris Williams would know Jake. 'Jennifer Bell. News and features writer for the *Chronicle*; a London newspaper.'

'How fascinating,' Chris enthused, taking the seat next to hers. 'Are you down here for a story or just for pleasure?'

'I've come to see Jake Richardson and do a follow-up story on his wife's suicide.' She watched for his reaction.

'Whew,' he whistled between his teeth. 'Have you now?' His glance at her was contemplative.

'Did you know her?' She took a sip of her drink, appraising him keenly over the rim of her glass.

'Yes, both her and Jake. Very sad business; very sad. Such a lovely woman. What a waste.'

'Quite. I'd really like to know what made her do it. Any ideas?

'Good grief, no. When I say I knew her, I meant as an acquaintance, that's all. It's Jake that I've had more dealings with.'

Jennifer waited but he didn't elaborate, so she went on, 'I've already been out to Peacock House – to see him.'

Chris's eyes widened at her. 'I would imagine you were about as welcome as a gumboil.'

Jennifer laughed at that. 'Something like that.'

'Did he agree to talk to you?'

'Oh yes – reluctantly, it has to be said.' She refrained from telling him that Jake has asked her to leave.

'I can imagine.' He laughed lightly. 'What did you think?'

Jennifer eyed him. 'Of what?'

'Of his lordship.'

'By that, I take it you mean Jake Richardson?'

Chris nodded. 'Not exactly the grieving husband, eh?'

'No.'

'I rang him – when I first heard the news of Esther's death. I wouldn't say he was rude . . . but. . . .' He shook his fingers in the air, indicating extreme trepidation.

Jennifer laughed again. 'Yes, he was a little abrupt today but I suppose that's understandable. He didn't seem to have much time for journalists – or anyone even remotely connected with a newspaper.' Her tone was acerbic and dry.

'No? Well, don't take it personally. Jake doesn't have much time for anybody.'

'Not even his wife?' she asked guilelessly.

Chris laughed lightly. 'I wouldn't know about that. He's always been a bit of a loner. Must have something to do with his being a writer. Still,' his glance now was distinctly appreciative, 'I'd have thought he'd have made time for someone who looks like you.'

Jennifer ignored that, going on to ask, 'You say you've had dealings with Mr Richardson. Just how well do you know him, Mr Williams?'

'Oh, call me Chris – please.'

He was an incorrigible flirt, that was becoming more evident with every word he said. 'All right, Chris. How well do you know Jake Richardson?'

'I know him solely as a business associate. He purchases the larger proportion of my imported wines and cheese – for his supermarkets. He's my main customer'.

'I see. So you knew Esther, you say, but not very well?'

'We used to meet now and again. You know, local social functions. She was a member of the same yacht club as me, sat on the carnival committee – that sort of thing.'

'Did she seem . . . troubled in any way before her suicide?'

'No. But then as I said, I hardly knew her so I doubt

if I would have noticed.'

'Did she have any close friends? Women who would have noticed – or that she might have confided in?'

'Well, there was one but I don't know whether she was a close friend. Janey Wilson. I believe they had lunch together sometimes. They played golf together, I do know that. I'm a member of the same club and I've seen them there several times. They always seemed chatty enough. You could ask her.'

'Where would I find her?'

'She owns a dress shop in Fore Street. "Janey's Gowns". She's there most of the time.

'Why so interested in Esther? She's nobody of any importance – well, other than being the wife of the great and good Jake Richardson, I suppose. I know the papers had a field day at the time but it's been almost six months now. Would your readers still be interested?'

'Oh, yes. It's a story of immense human interest plus, as you say, she's the wife of a famous writer. I'm sure our readers will find it fascinating. What drove a woman, who on the surface had everything – a handsome husband, a beautiful daughter, plenty of money, a super home – to put an end to her existence in a small town hotel? Hmmm? It has all the ingredients of an Alfred Hitchcock film. But that aside, what I'm really interested in, and my editor is the same, is how have the family coped since? What developments have there been?'

'Yes, I see.'

'How well do you know Lucy's nurse, Pauline Duvall?

'Hey, what is this?' Chris laughed. 'This is more of

an interrogation than an interview.' He raised his two hands in submission. 'Not guilty, m'lud.'

'Sorry. It's my journalist's nosc working overtime, I'm afraid. You'll have to forgive me.'

'That's OK. I don't know Pauline anywhere near as well as I'd like to.' He gave an exaggerated leer at Jennifer's raised eyebrows. 'No, only kidding. I think she's spoken for actually, ' he concluded, lightheartedly.

'Oh? By whom?' Jennifer's pulses quickened, her instincts telling her that she was on to something. But disappointingly, all Chris would vouchsafe was an intriguingly wicked, 'That's all I'm going to say. If I'm wrong and word gets about, it's my head that's on the chopping block for opening my big mouth.

'Can I buy you another drink, Jennifer?'

And that was that. Jennifer couldn't get him to say anything else. She was pretty sure to what he was alluding, though. Jake Richardson and Pauline Duvall.

She had to find out more. She'd go and see Janey Wilson first thing tomorrow.

# Five

But when, the following morning, Jennifer came out of breakfast it was to discover Jake and Lucy sitting in the reception area, upon one of the comfortable settees, clearly awaiting her. She'd have to postpone her visit to Janey's Gowns, for the moment, at least.

'Jennifer!' Lucy called.

'Please be quiet, Lucy.' Jennifer heard Jake remonstrate. 'There are other guests to be taken into consideration.'

Jennifer saw the child's face fall and all her antipathy of the previous day towards Jake Richardson returned, in full force.

'Hello, Lucy,' she greeted the little girl as she walked towards the two people, her warm smile meant for the child alone. She held out a welcoming hand and Lucy, making no secret of her pleasure in seeing Jennifer again, skipped over and seized it. 'What are you doing here?'

'We've come to get you, Jennifer.'

Jennifer's gaze darted to the face of the man standing quietly to one side of them. Unsmiling, he returned Jennifer's glance.

'Come to get me? What do you mean?' Jennifer tried to keep her tone unconcerned but she had a strong suspicion that she didn't succeed.

'You really should have come clean with me, Jennifer, before confiding in Lucy,' Jake put in, quietly.

Jennifer found herself trembling slightly at the glint that invaded the dark eyes as he spoke. His voice seemed to throb deep in this throat. It endowed her name with an unusual attractiveness.

'Aah.' Jake was, of course, referring to her conversation with his daughter and the fact that she had told Lucy that she had once known Esther.

'Why didn't you say that you knew my wife? That you were friends? Instead of coming out with all that nonsense about being here for a story?'

'It's not nonsense,' Jennifer protested indignantly. 'I am here for a story. Esther and I did know each other but – well, it was a long time ago . . . and we sort of lost touch. . . .' Her words tailed off lamely.

'Why was that?'

'We just drifted apart, I guess.'

'You and I have never met, have we?'

Jennifer shook her head.'

'And I don't recall Esther ever having mentioned a Jennifer Bell. There was one girl that she talked about now and again, I believe they kept in touch. Kathy Bellamy. Did you know her? Funnily enough, she's a writer as well.' His glance sharpened then. And for a moment, Jennifer wondered if he'd seen through her deception.

'I didn't know her very well,' Jennifer lied, crossing her fingers behind her back as she did so.

'Is that why you decided to do the follow-up feature on Esther? Because of your long-ago friendship?'

'Well, it was partly that, I must confess, but it was initially my editor's idea. He doesn't know that I knew Esther.'

'It must have been a considerable shock to you. To hear of her death?'

'Yes, it was.'

He was contemplating her thoughtfully now. 'So you haven't spoken to Esther in recent times at all?'

'No, I told you; we lost touch. And in any case, I was abroad at the time of her . . . .' She smiled weakly at him. Suddenly she couldn't seem to bring herself to mention her friend's death. 'I was in Bosnia – Sarajevo – when it happened.'

'What on earth were you doing there?' He looked surprised. Probably didn't think a mere woman was up to the task of entering war-torn Bosnia and reporting back on it, she mused sourly. He obviously hadn't heard of Kate Adie!

'My job!' she riposted smartly. 'I was engaged upon a series of weekly reports on the plight of the orphan children and the dreadful conditions in which they were living – if you could call it living, that is.'

'I see. I was hoping that if you had communicated, Esther might have given you some hint of what was bothering her sufficiently to drive her to suicide.'

'I would have thought, Mr Richardson, that, as her husband, you would have known that.' She went on smoothly, 'Surely if something were really wrong. . . .'

His head jerked up and his eyes narrowed at her, making him appear almost menacing – dangerous.

'What are you implying?' he demanded quietly. 'That she would kill herself on a whim?'

'No, of course not.'

'Mind you, knowing Esther, it wouldn't have been beyond the bounds of possibility. She was always the one for the melodramatic gesture. . . .' He directed a wry smile her way.

Jennifer didn't reciprocate. Instead, her tone was sharp with sarcasm. 'To the point of downing a bottle of red wine and a lethal dose of sleeping pills? A bit melodramatic even for Esther. Especially as she was pregnant. I would have thought she had everything to live for.'

Once again, Jake Richardson's eyes narrowed at her.

A sudden suspicion visited Jennifer. 'You didn't know, at the time, that she was pregnant, did you?'

'No. I doubt she'd known long herself.'

'Strange though – that she didn't tell you; her husband?'

There was a short silence and then Jake said, 'Not really. Esther and I. . . .'

'Jennifer.'

They'd both forgotten Lucy standing patiently to one side, still clinging to Jennifer's hand. She tugged upon her fingers now.

'I'm sorry, darling, Jennifer bent down to the child, 'we'd quite forgotten you were there.' Which was an understandable oversight upon Jennifer's part; upon a father's, however, it wasn't so understandable. The more she knew of this man and his child, the more convinced she became that Lucy could be right. He didn't want her around. Jennifer's heart ached for the little girl. She gave Lucy a hug, all the time speculating on what it was that Jake had been about to say then. 'What is it? Hmmm?'

'You're coming to stay with us. Daddy said you could.'

Jennifer glanced up at Jake. Her shock must have been evident upon her face because there was an even more visible glint to Jake's eye now as he returned her stare. She straightened, although she kept a hand upon Lucy's shoulder.

'Well.' He did smile then, a genuine smile of amusement – even if it was from between tightened lips. 'As usual my daughter has pre-empted me.'

'Oh!' Jennifer didn't know what to say. An invitation to stay at Peacock House was the very last thing she had expected. Truth to tell, she didn't know if she wanted to stay there – with this narrow-eyed, enigmatic man. Yet – it would give her a chance to have a good look through Esther's things, to search for any possible clues to Esther's state of mind before her death. She could also keep her eye upon Jake and Pauline Duvall, maybe confirm that they were indeed indulging in an affair thus provoking the despair and possible fear of desertion by her husband that had driven Esther to the lengths of taking her own life. But if that were the case why hadn't they married? And what possible motive could Jake Richardson have for inviting her to stay – in his house?

'Well, if you don't object, Mr Richardson. . . .'

'Oh, please. Call me Jake. We can't remain on such

formal terms if you're coming to stay with us, can we?' A curious expression glittered once more from the dark eyes. 'Lucy insists. She's taken a real fancy to you, Jennifer.'

The manner in which he said her name and the look that was to be seen in his eye suggested to Jennifer that he did indeed want her in his house. But for what reason Jennifer still had no notion.

'Would you like to settle your bill? You might as well return with us now. I've got the car outside.'

And so, that's exactly what Jennifer did. It was overwhelmingly evident that Jake Richardson was accustomed to getting his own way – over everything. She'd glimpsed no anticipation of her refusal to accept his invitation. He'd never for a moment doubted but that he only had to say the word and she would leap to do his bidding. Jennifer's lips pursed in annoyance. She should have refused to go along with his wishes. However, it was too late now; she'd accepted. She went upstairs and obediently packed her case with Lucy at her side, chattering constantly throughout.

Upon her arrival at Peacock House, the housekeeper, Mrs Elliot, showed her to a lovely bedroom with an en-suite bathroom, its windows overlooking the extensive gardens to the rear of the house. In the distance, she could hear the boom-boom of the waves as they broke upon the rocks at the foot of the cliffs.

'Did you know Mrs Richardson?' the housekeeper asked.

'A long time ago. This is a lovely house. I love the stone peacocks; they're a work of art in themselves, aren't they? Who sculpted them, do you know. . . ?'

But the housekeeper obviously wasn't to be distracted by trivia. She asked, 'You're here to write a feature on her, aren't you?'

'Yes.'

'I heard the call that night, you know.' She looked almost nervous for a second as she glanced back at Jennifer.

'Call? What call?'

'The call of the peacock.'

Jennifer, her journalistic tendencies coming to the fore, waited for her to go on.

'They always screech when a death is imminent. The death of someone in the family, that is. An unnatural death. They screamed that night. I heard them.'

'Do you mean the night that Mrs Richardson died?'

'Yes.'

'But . . . ' Jennifer was puzzled, 'There are no live peacocks here anymore, are there?'

'No'

'Then how . . . ? I don't understand.'

'They've always been heard then – ever since there were live ones and an ancestor of Mr Richardson's was murdered. They were heard crying all night before his death . . . . The widow got rid of them then and there've been no live ones here since. She reckoned they'd been some sort of omen and she wouldn't have them round her any more . . . . Then they were heard to cry before Mr Richardson's grandfather died even though there were none around.'

'How did he die?'

'Hunting accident. Fell from his horse and broke his neck. I'm telling you, as sure as I'm standing here, I heard them that night?'

'But – but you were out, weren't you – that night?'

'Only for the evening, Miss Bell. I came back round about eleven-thirty, maybe twelve o'clock, I didn't check the clock right away, and it was then that I heard them . . . .' She shuddered. 'It was that eerie. Frightened me to death I can tell you. There weren't no one in the house but me, you see . . . .'

'How did you know that Mrs Richardson wasn't at home? As far as you knew, surely, she could have returned earlier and gone to bed?'

'Oh no, Miss Bell. I knew she wasn't back. Her car wasn't parked outside. If she came back late at night, she always left it out the front. Said she didn't like going round the back to the garages. No lights round there, you see.'

'But it was late. Didn't you wonder where Mrs Richardson was?'

'No, she'd told me she wouldn't be back till late. She often went out while Mr Richardson was away. I never thought anything of it. I went to bed, so I didn't know that she hadn't returned till morning. And even then, I didn't really think anything of it. I just assumed she'd stayed with friends. She sometimes did – if she'd had a bit too much to drink to drive back or the weather was particularly bad – which it was that night.'

'Did she ever tell you where she went on these outings?'

'No and it weren't my place to ask.' The woman seemed to stiffen momentarily, eyeing Jennifer, her expression guarded.

So, there had been no possibility of Mrs Elliot checking up on Esther that last night. Esther must have known that. So, in that case, why had she gone to the hotel?

'She had friends in Truro, I believe. Mebbe she went there. She didn't like being in the house alone.'

'But normally you would have been here, and Miss Duvall, surely?'

'Oh, we didn't count.' There was the faintest trace of bitterness to the housekeeper's tone now. Jennifer wondered why.

'Mr Richardson took the nurse and Lucy with him to London that day, didn't he? And they all stayed overnight.'

'Yes.'

'Does he often do that?' Jennifer deliberately kept her tone casual. She didn't want the woman to feel she was being interrogated. 'You know, take Lucy and the nurse when he goes away?'

The woman eyed her. 'You've been reading them reports of a love triangle, haven't you? You don't want to pay no attention to them. No, he didn't normally take them. I do know that he had to see someone up there, in London – about Lucy,' she added, obviously as an afterthought, 'but about what, I've really no idea. I don't ask questions, Miss Bell, it's not my place. I'm just the housekeeper here.'

Once Jennifer had unpacked, she went to the phone that she had seen in the hallway downstairs to ring David and tell him where she was. She also wanted to tell him that she was using the name of Jennifer Bell. She had hoped to have a phone in her bedroom. This was one call she needed to make in privacy. However, a swift glance round told her that she was alone so picking up the receiver she dialled David's work number.

She was put through to him straight away and lost no time in relaying the day's events. She had just said, 'By the way, if you should need to get in touch with me, I'm known here as Jennifer Bell . . .' when she became aware of someone standing to one side and behind her. She swung quickly, to see – Jake. He was standing in an open doorway on the other side of the hallway, watching her over the rim of a cup. Jennifer turned back to the phone and said, 'David, I'll have to go. I'll ring in a day or two.'

When she had replaced the receiver, she swung slowly to discover Jake still watching her. Had he heard?

But Jake gave no sign that he'd heard her words, instead holding his cup up in the air, he said, 'Fancy a cup of coffee?'

'Love one.'

'Come in here then,' Jake invited, leading the way into a truly sumptuous lounge. French windows stood open to the sunshine and the garden. It was a beautiful morning. The air was crystal clear and the scents of the many flowers in bloom were drifting in, perfuming the room with the distinctive smell of summertime. The scream of wheeling seagulls and the distant boom-boom of the waves were the only sounds to break the silence as Jake poured the coffee into a delicate porcelain cup.

Without looking at her, Jake spoke. 'Your editor was that?'

'No.'

He stood up and walked across the pale green carpet towards her, balancing the cup and saucer in his hand. Jennifer took it, carefully avoiding the brush of his fingers. She was becoming increasingly disturbed by Jake. He watched her through narrowed eyes.

'Oh?' He didn't actually ask the question but it hung in the air between them.

'He's – a friend.'

'Is that all? Just a friend?' Jake's one eyebrow had lifted, it bestowed a devilish, attractive air upon him. He'd obviously noted her hesitation.

She didn't know what made her say what she said next. 'As far as I'm concerned, yes.' Although what business it is of yours . . . ? she wanted to add. She didn't though. There was no purpose to be served in deliberately tweaking the tiger's tail. She smiled to herself. That was a remarkably appropriate simile for Jake Richardson. He did indeed resemble a beast of prey. Lithe, powerful, there was an air of sleek purposefulness about him. She wouldn't care to be the one that he marked down as his quarry.

'Something amusing you?' he suddenly asked. His dark eyes gleamed at her over the rim of his cup.

'It's nothing. A private joke,' she hastened to add in the face of his obvious scepticism. He was too perceptive by half. That fact alone could make her stay here fraught with peril. If he uncovered the truth – that she was the Kathy Bellamy that he had spoken of . . . ? In direct contrast to her earlier resolve to keep the secret of her identity, she realized that she should have owned up when he invited her to his house.

'Well, why don't you share it?'

'Oh no, it's much too private.'

He didn't say anything else, although his eyes remained fixed upon her as he lazily sipped his coffee. Jennifer lifted her cup to her mouth then as well and took a sip of the hot, delicious liquid. She looked about the room, looking for something to say that would defuse the tension that had suddenly arisen between them. 'What a charming room this is,' she belatedly and rather naively blurted out, only to feel distinctly foolish when she saw the manner in which Jake's beautifully shaped mouth quirked upward at the corners.

'Yes, isn't it?' he murmured sardonically. 'And such beautiful paintings and ornaments. And the view from those windows is truly spectacular . . . .' He lazily indicated the French windows behind him. 'So, now that the courtesies are dispensed with . . . .' He smiled provocatively and Jennifer glanced back at him, only to think for the umpteenth time, what a handsome man Jake Richardson was. She bit her bottom lip. She was proving every bit as susceptible as every other woman probably was, she mused in some irritation. Jake Richardson possessed an inherent attraction for the opposite sex. She hadn't been able to help noticing the various women who had been standing around the reception hall of The Smuggler's Arms looking at him. Jake himself, she had to admit, hadn't seemed to perceive the response that he had aroused. But, nonetheless, to a woman, they had preened themselves, making no secret of their hopes that he would glance their way. And here she was, proving no better than the very females that she professed to despise.

'Do you want to talk about Esther?' Jake was now saying. 'I was very rude yesterday morning – the manner in which I dismissed you. Please accept my apologies. You were only doing your job after all. I'd like to make amends if I can.'

Jennifer regarded him, astonished by the deep feelings of guilt that assailed her. She really should tell him the truth. Both who she was and that she was here – under instruction to dig up whatever she could about the weeks before Esther's death with a view to discovering precisely who or what had driven her to suicide. Even if it should be found that he was the guilty party because of his affair with the lovely Pauline. What would he do, once he knew her intentions? Jennifer suspected that he wouldn't be so keen to talk about Esther. In fact, she wouldn't mind betting that he'd go so far as to ask her to leave again.

Better to say nothing – for the moment at any rate. If circumstances changed, well – then she'd rethink the situation. It was to Esther that her loyalties lay, she reaffirmed; not her husband. And after all, she'd be gone again in a very short while – once she'd discovered what had driven her friend to suicide. For her own peace of mind now, if for nothing else, she needed to uncover the truth.

# Six

'Yes, I would like to talk about Esther – if you don't mind,' Jennifer agreed.

'When was the last time you saw her?' Suddenly, it seemed to be Jake asking the questions. Jennifer smiled to herself. Never mind. Could be that she'd find out more from casual conversation than she would from a more formalized interview.

'Over five years ago. Before Lucy was born. I came here to see her once or twice. You were away on business.'

Jennifer was deliberately vague. He most likely knew about her visits but under the name of Katherine Bellamy. They had been timed on both occasions to fit in with his absences – at Esther's instigation. She had wondered at the time if Jake hadn't liked his wife seeing her old friends.

'Yes, I was doing a good bit of travelling around then

both for my research for my books and to buy for my supermarkets. I've managed to cut down on that though, at least, as far as the buying goes. Chris Williams has the problems now instead of me,' he smiled grimly. 'I still have to travel for my writing, of course.'

'I met him last night,' she slipped in casually. She was curious about his attitude towards Chris.

'You did? Where?'

'He came into the hotel for a drink. We had a chat. He does business there as well, I gather.'

'What did you think of him?'

Jennifer smiled to herself. Chris had asked her the same question. Why did she get the distinct impression that the two men had no liking for each other?

'I liked him.'

'Yes,' Jake drawled drily, 'most women do – my wife was no exception. He has a little-boy charm, she once informed me.'

Jennifer eyed him.

'Oh, it's all right, you needn't look at me like that. He and I get along all right – as long as he does his job. That's what I pay him for.' There was more than a trace of hauteur in Jake's voice now. 'So,' he changed the subject,'how did you and Esther manage to lose touch so completely?'

She shrugged. 'Our ways parted. She married you and moved down here. I stayed in London and eventually began to travel for the paper.'

'You said you came for the odd visit though.'

'Yes.' She was again deliberately vague. 'As I said, my work took me further and further afield. Esther became more involved with the local community here. . . .'

'You're not married, Jennifer . . . .'

His glance shifted to her left hand and her bare third finger.

The way that he said her name, deep in his throat, once again dispatched a ripple of – what? she asked herself furiously, excitement? It couldn't be. Why, she didn't even like the man. Nonetheless, she found herself wondering how it would sound, whispered in love – or passion?

'No.' Her response sounded stilted in the aftermath of her shocking reflections – even to her own ears.

Jake's gaze absorbed her faint blush and her pursed lips. 'The men in your vicinity blind or something?' The question was so quietly asked that she wondered for a second if she'd misheard him.

Despite her astonishment, however, her gaze remained level as it met with his.

'I wouldn't know. Up till now I've never met a man that I've wanted to spend my life with . . . .' Her words petered out as she realized the interpretation that he could, and probably would – knowing him – place upon her guileless words.

But he seemed not to have noticed her slip. Or had he? she wondered uncomfortably. There was a strange expression in his eyes as he continued to regard her. One of almost tender amusement.

'What? Not even your David?'

'He's not my David,' she curtly responded.

'Does he know that?' Jake appeared utterly relaxed as he leant back in his chair, with one foot propped casually upon his other knee. A complete contrast to her, Jennifer decided. She felt like a cat on a hot tin roof. Was this the effect he had on everyone? Most likely, she reflected somewhat bitterly. Especially upon his female acquaintances.

'I thought we were here to discuss Esther, not my affairs . . . .' She bit her lip. As she had decided only the day before, he had the most unusual effect upon her. All of her customary common sense and level headedness seemed to have deserted her. Just by using the word 'affairs' she would lead him to believe she was deceiving him about David. Which, of course, she was – to a certain extent. It was a disquieting notion. For two pins, she'd leave this house and Trezillian straight away. She had no liking for deceit – or treachery – and here she was practising both. Why, oh why, hadn't she held out against him and Lucy and remained at the hotel?

He didn't seem the least bit put out by her abruptness with him. Instead of biting back as she half expected, he simply said, 'Fire ahead then. What do you want to know?'

'Did she help you with your writing at all?'

'No. I don't recall her ever reading any of my books even.'

'What about the supermarkets? Did she . . . . ?'

'No.'

'She devoted herself to Lucy and the home, did she?' It seemed the logical conclusion to draw in the face of Jake's repeatedly negative answers, although, even to Jennifer, that didn't sound like the Esther she recalled.

'No.' Jake allowed himself a small smile at his third no in a row. 'We employ a housekeeper and a nurse. You've met both of them.'

'Yes' She didn't want to get drawn on the subject of

either the housekeeper or Pauline Duvall. She'd reserve the subject of Pauline until such time as she was more sure of her ground. Or when she had some substantiation of her suspicions of a romantic affair between them. 'But surely Esther took some part in rearing Lucy?'

'No, she didn't. Esther wasn't the maternal type. I would have thought, as her friend, you would have known that.' He seemed amused again.

'Well – yes, of course I did – but Esther was longing for Lucy's arrival the last time I saw her.'

'Oh, she was – till Lucy arrived. Then the reality didn't fit in with Esther's idealized notions of motherhood. Too much mess, too much responsibility, too many disturbances to the smooth running of her life ....' He shrugged. 'I'm a relatively wealthy man – it seemed much the best – for Lucy and for Esther – to simply employ a nurse. Then everyone was happy.'

Jennifer stared at him. Had he really thought that? Just a few words with Lucy had revealed that child's discontent and insecurity. And as for Esther – well, Esther certainly wouldn't have committed suicide if she'd been happy. It was true that Esther had always taken the easy way out of any situation but surely as she grew and matured she would have seen that life wasn't always that simple? Or was Jake deliberately blackening her character? To excuse his own infidelity? Yet, and she couldn't deny it, even Lucy had said she didn't see much of her mother.

'I see.'

'Do you? I have a feeling that you wouldn't shirk the responsibilities of motherhood and marriage, Jennifer. Tell me. Do they come into your plans for the future?

Perhaps with the mysterious David?'

Jennifer felt ridiculously pleased by his belief that she wasn't afraid of responsibility. So much so, that she found herself blushing again. What was wrong with her? This interview wasn't going as she had planned at all. Deciding to change tack before the situation got completely out of hand, she decided to ignore those last questions and asked, 'But was Esther happy? Surely if she had been, she wouldn't have . . . ?'

'Committed suicide? No. Esther wasn't particularly happy – or so she told me at any rate.' He smiled grimly at her.

'Why not?' She decided to go in hard with her questions and see what results she got this time. He could hardly throw her out again, not right after inviting her to stay.

'I wasn't doting enough – or that's what she told me. I didn't dance attendance upon her as she would have liked, lavish her with the right sort of gifts – oh, you don't want to hear all this.'

'Did you try and make her happy?'

'Yes, of course I did.' Jake got to his feet and strode to the open French window. He stood, with his back to Jennifer, staring out. 'But after a while I gave up on it. It was an impossible task and I'm afraid I'm not the sort of man to sacrifice everything to a woman's demands. I couldn't give her what she wanted so . . . .' He shrugged his shoulders and still not turning lapsed into a brooding silence. 'I gave up even trying. We'd lived relatively separate lives for the last couple of years.'

'What did she do with herself then?'

'Nothing much apart from socialize with her various friends. Sit on committees. Raise money for this, that and the other. Anything but what I asked of her. To be a wife to me and a mother to her child.'

'Her child?

'Sorry.' Jake's response was terse as he swung and looked at Jennifer again. 'Our child.'

More and more, it was beginning to seem that Lucy was right. Her father did dislike her. But why? Lucy had seemed a perfectly normal child to Jennifer. Brighter than most, certainly.

Mind you, she decided cynically, all of this could explain Jake's need for an extra-marital affair. Or affairs? But surely, he couldn't be blaming Lucy for her mother's inadequacies as a wife? Another notion occurred to Jennifer at that. If Esther had realized that he was thinking this way, felt that way about Lucy, and knowing that she was pregnant again with a child that, possibly, her husband wouldn't welcome, would it have been sufficient to inspire her to commit suicide? It seemed unlikely but she'd already been unhappy because – in Jake's words 'he hadn't danced attendance on her.' If he had told her that as far as he was concerned the marriage was over – which was all Jennifer could deduce from his comment about their separate lives – would that, perhaps coupled with her fear of giving him a second unwanted child, have driven her to such desperate lengths? But, all that aside, Jennifer couldn't escape the fact that Esther had been pregnant which did seem to indicate that there had been some degree of intimacy between husband and wife. Perhaps she was making too much of Jake's comments. After all, it wasn't uncommon today for couples to lead fairly separate lives. Perhaps Esther's suicide had nothing to do with any of this.

Suddenly Jennifer couldn't go on with the interview. Not for the moment. She needed time to digest all that Jake had told her.

'Do you mind if we leave this for now, Jake? I have to go out.' She needed another viewpoint. It might put Jake's views upon his wife into some sort of perspective. She would do what she'd intended to do earlier and go and see Janey Wilson.

'No, I've got an appointment anyway – in half an hour.' As Jake spoke he'd lifted his shirt cuff and revealed a slender gold wristwatch. More evidence of his immense wealth. It looked like a very expensive watch indeed.

Jennifer slipped her notepad and pen into her handbag and left the house. She decided to walk into the town. She needed the fresh air. It might help her to clear her head and put her thoughts into some semblance of order.

Trezillian was a medium-sized, seaside town, its pretty pastel painted houses clinging to the side of a steep hill that ran directly down to the sea and the picturesque harbour. It had been a sizeable fishing port at one time but with the decline in the fishing industry it had turned its attention to the holiday trade. Now two large caravan parks more or less encircled the town and the erstwhile fishing boats ran coastal trips for the holiday makers. It contained a number of guest houses but with the advent of the caravan parks, only one hotel, The Smuggler's Arms.

Jennifer decided to try and glean some information from one or two of the local residents about Esther and Jake's life together. She had an uneasy suspicion that Jake wasn't being altogether honest with her.

Her first port of call was the small shop-cum-post office. Jennifer had always found that one of the most valuable sources of information in any village or modestly sized town. On the pretence of buying stamps and a map of the surrounding area, she managed to let it be known that she was a guest at Peacock House, visiting with the intention of doing a feature on Esther for a London newspaper.

The middle-aged woman behind the counter blinked at her for a moment or two before demanding, in the forthright manner that she was beginning to believe was a general characteristic of the people hereabouts, 'Hasn't Mr Richardson been able to tell you all you want?'

'I really wanted to get some local information about her. You know, what she did for the benefit of the local community, that sort of thing. How the inhabitants of Trezillian felt about her . . . . ?'

'Well, I wouldn't say people felt anything about her. The ordinary folk didn't really know her. She didn't do an awful lot for the town. She was always busy – or looked it, at least.' She sniffed. 'Rushing here, there and everywhere. I believe she helped out on the carnival committee. You know, organizing fund raising events and the like, her and that Janey Wilson. But they both consider – well, considered in Mrs Richardson's case themselves a cut above everybody else. Mind you,' she sniffed again, 'he . . . .' she paused significantly, clearly referring to Jake, 'didn't spend much time at home. Stands to reason she'd look elsewhere for company.'

'I see,' Jennifer paused. 'And where exactly did she look for that company?'

The woman sniffed again and this time there was no mistaking her disapproval – but whether it was of Jake or Esther, Jennifer would have been hard put to say. 'That's all I'm saying. It doesn't do to speak ill of the dead – or anyone else, come to that.' And she frowned repressively at the by now openly puzzled Jennifer.

Jennifer paid for the stamps and the map and took herself off. That was something that she hadn't previously considered – that Esther might have had someone else. A lover. It gave a whole new dimension to the matter. Her next call was upon Janey Wilson. Janey proved friendly enough even if she did eye her rather cautiously at Jennifer's request for an interview about Esther.

'I don't know that I can really tell you very much. We played golf together on Wednesday and Sunday mornings then usually had lunch at the club but Esther . . . .' She looked uncomfortable here, 'well, I don't mean to speak ill of the dead but Esther was a very shallow woman. She lived for the moment and blow the consequences.'

'So she didn't talk to you about her home life – with her husband and little girl?'

'Good heavens – no.'

'Would you have described Mrs Richardson as a happy woman?'

'Well ... yes – although . . .' Janey paused, as if unsure whether to continue or not 'that last month – you know, just before she died – she seemed different – now that you ask.'

'In what way?'

'She grew very tetchy, impatient. As if she were waiting for something, you know? Yes, that's the only way I can describe it. Waiting for something.'

'So she never talked about her husband, Jake Richardson?'

'Only to mention him in passing – as one does. I got the impression they weren't really happy together, though.'

Jennifer looked politely enquiring.

'Well, Mr Richardson was away from home a good deal and it left her alone in that great house, apart from the housekeeper, Mrs Elliot, and the child's nurse, um, Pauline somebody or other.'

'Her name's Duvall.'

'That's it, Duvall. I don't know what Esther did with herself half the time – especially in the winter months. Apart from the yacht club and her golfing activities, she wasn't seen much locally. I always assumed her friends lived further afield – her real friends, that is. She didn't ever mention anyone though, now that I come to consider it.'

'What was Mrs Richardson's relationship with Lucy's nurse, Pauline Duvall? They must have been about the same age.'

Janey looked thoughtful. 'She never really mentioned her.'

'Did Mrs Richardson ever stay away overnight anywhere – leaving her husband at home with Miss Duvall?'

Janey regarded Jennifer askance now. 'You mean those newspaper reports – of something going on between Mr Richardson and Pauline? No, never. There was never the slightest suggestion of anything like that. Pauline's a lovely looking woman, I have to say that, but I wouldn't have thought she was Jake's type. Too cold.' She seemed strangely vehement about the idea and as Jennifer stared at her, a blush coloured her skin pink and her gaze dropped away. 'She comes into the shop now and again, so I know what I'm talking about.'

So, – all of a sudden, it was Jake, was it? Not Mr Richardson. Had she been barking up the wrong tree all along? And after all, it wouldn't be the first time a frustrated husband had strayed to one of his wife's friends.

'And what is – Jake's,' she subtly emphasized the word '"type"?'

'Well,' Janey gave a high, embarrassed titter, 'how on earth would I know? But he's a handsome man. Half of the female population to Trezillian, given the opportunity, would welcome his advances.'

'I see.' And Jennifer did. Even if Jake didn't return the compliment, Janey Wilson fancied him like mad.

'Look, I must get on, Miss Bell. I've got all of these blouses to sort and price,' she indicated a pile of garments sitting on the counter 'before I go home for lunch. It's my half-day closing so I want to get away on time.'

'Well, if you think of anything, any little detail, that might enrich my article about Mrs Richardson perhaps you'd let me know. I'm staying at Peacock House.' She only just managed to suppress her amusement at the chagrined expression that crossed Janey Wilson's face at that piece of information 'Mr Richardson – Jake – very kindly asked me to stay.'

Jennifer decided after that that she'd pay a visit to The Smuggler's Arms and treat herself to a pot of coffee and a cake. The manager was standing at the desk in the reception hall.

'Aah, Miss Bell,' he drawled smoothly. 'How nice to

see you back. Forget something, did you?

Jennifer thought she detected an undertone of malice beneath the outwardly gracious words. She directed a piercing glance his way. Had she imagined it? Or was he annoyed because she'd left his hotel and moved into Peacock House? As ridiculous as that seemed it was the only reason she could come up with for such strange behaviour.

'No. I wondered if I might get a pot of coffee? The only cafe doesn't seem to be open.'

'Yes, of course.' Now she couldn't mistake the relief in the man's tone. What did he think she'd come in for? 'If you go into the lounge, I'll have it sent in to you.'

'Thank you. Um . . . you knew Esther Richardson, didn't you?'

'Ye . . . es.'

'I believe she often came here for a drink?'

His glance slid away from hers now. 'I wouldn't say – often. She came in now and again. She never stopped long,' he added.

'Didn't you think it odd for her to arrive and take a room on the evening of her suicide?'

'I don't ask my guests why they want a room, Miss Bell. Especially not when they are the wife of a prominent local businessman.'

'What reason did she give?'

'I don't know that she did give one. It's none of our business after all.'

'Who would have checked her in?'

'Look, I've been through all of this with the police. I really can't see that it's anyone else's concern.'

Jennifer gave a non-committal smile. 'Did she meet anyone here?'

The manager drew himself up. 'I have no idea,' he retorted in a lofty manner. 'Now, I'll go and see to your coffee – if you will excuse me.' He gave a stiff little bow and hurriedly made his exit. Jennifer stood, looking after him for a second before she strolled into the lounge.

A young woman brought her coffee. She checked out the badge that the girl wore on her blouse lapel. Elaine Blair, Receptionist.

'Miss Blair,' Jennifer began, 'I wonder if you can help me. I'm from the *Chronicle* – a London paper – and I'm doing a feature on Esther Richardson. You know the sort of thing – how she'll be missed, a kind of memorial to her.' She gave the girl a deliberately warm smile. 'I'm looking for some background material on events leading up to the tragedy as well as what's happened since.'

The girl's hands were noticeably trembling as she placed the tray upon the table.

'Did you book Mrs Richardson into the hotel on that last evening?'

'Yes,' the girl muttered.

'Why was she here? Did she say?'

The girl shook her head. 'No.'

'Didn't you think it strange that she should book a room when she lived not far away?'

The girl shrugged. 'Well, it wasn't a very nice night so perhaps she didn't fancy venturing out again.'

'Was she planning to meet someone, do you know?'

'I have no idea. I can only tell you what I told the police. I didn't see her with anyone. She was certainly alone when she checked in.'

'Had she ever taken a room here before?'

'No, not that I know of. But then I'm not always on duty.'

'But surely you must have thought it unusual that she did so that night?'

'It's not my place to think anything.'

'So no one joined her later?'

'Not as far as I knew. Sorry, I'm frightfully busy – must go.'

Jennifer watched as the girl practically ran from the room. She poured herself a cup of coffee. Esther had met someone here that night. She'd lay money on that. But who had it been? A man? And if that were the case, why was no one at the hotel saying so?

'Jennifer.'

Jennifer glanced up. Chris Williams stood looking down at her.

'Any coffee to spare in that?' He indicated the coffee pot.

'Yes, of course.' She poured him a cup of the fragrant black liquid. 'What are you doing here?'

'Bit of business. Robert, the manager, buys his wines and cheeses for the hotel from me. Not in the quantities that Jake does, of course, but every little bit helps these days. He said you were in here.'

The brown eyes staring into hers darkened and Jennifer wondered what Robert had told him.

'I was wondering, Jennifer, if you'd fancy having a meal with me one evening?'

'I'd love to.' Chris Williams was a very attractive man, so it would be no hardship to spend some time with him.

'Monday evening? Eight o'clock – here?'

'Fine.'

'Um I wouldn't mention our date to Jake, by the way.'

Puzzled, Jennifer considered his request. 'Why ever not?'

'He doesn't believe in mixing business with pleasure. I hear you're staying at his place. He likes to keep his personal life very much separate from his business affairs. He might object to us seeing each other.'

'Well, I can't see that it's any of his concern what I do but if that's what you want, OK.'

'Right. That's settled then. I must fly. Monday night it is then. Don't forget.'

'I won't.' Her gaze followed him. Yes, he was a very attractive man. Suddenly, she found herself wishing their date had been fixed for that evening and not four nights hence. It would be a relief to get away from Peacock House and away from her memories of Esther and Jake Richardson's increasingly disturbing presence, even if it were only for a few hours.

From then on, Jennifer seemed only to encounter brick walls whenever she tried to find out more about Esther's last weeks. As Bill had remarked, no one seemed willing to talk about either Jake or his wife. She spent two fairly fruitless days and was beginning to despair of ever getting any further with her quest.

It was the next evening before Pauline Duvall joined Jake and Jennifer in the dining-room for dinner. From the time that Jennifer had arrived at Peacock House, she and Jake had dined alone and she had presumed that the nurse took her meals in her room. Whatever the reason for Pauline's continued absence, Jennifer had utilized the time with Jake to try and find out a little more about Esther but Jake had proved remarkably unforthcoming upon the subject of his wife. He'd seemed to prefer to talk about Jennifer and she'd found herself telling him of her work for the paper and of her travels in her capacity of foreign affairs correspondent. An unexpected rapport had begun to develop between them and once again, Jennifer discovered herself assailed by feelings of guilt about her masquerade. But upon this particular evening, once Lucy had been given her tea and finally was in bed, Pauline joined them. Lucy had wanted to share their meal and had, for once, resorted to tantrums to try and get her own way.

Jake had shown remarkable forbearance, Jennifer considered, taking into account his normal manner towards his daughter, but even he, eventually, had lost his cool and had snapped, 'Go to bed, Lucy, before you and I really fall out.'

'No,' Lucy had courageously defied him, 'I want to stay with Jennifer . . . .'

'Lucy,' Jake had warned darkly, 'if I have to raise my voice . . . .'

Strangely enough, Pauline Duvall had seemed to stand back and allow events to take their course which Jennifer deemed odd – since she was employed to take care of Lucy. Suddenly though, she said, 'Lucy, sweetheart, Daddy's right.' She then glanced at Jake, as if to say, 'See, you need me to look after her.'

Jennifer watched silently as Lucy finally gave in and with tears filling her eyes went with her nurse.

Jake then turned towards Jennifer and said, 'Sorry about all that. Her behaviour is worsening, the older she gets.' He gave a wry smile. 'I'd always assumed it would improve with age.'

'Well, she is only five,' Jennifer replied. 'And perhaps it's your attention she's really after. With her mother gone . . . .'

'She's going to have to learn that she can't always have my attention then, Jennifer.'

'That's a little hard, isn't it? She's. . . .'

'No,' Jake insisted, smoothly, 'it isn't. I'm not having her grow up, cast in the same mould as her mother. She'll have to learn. I have a business to run, as well as my books to write. I cannot spend every moment that she demands with her.'

'I'm sure she doesn't want every moment,' Jennifer responded quietly, 'just a few.'

Jake made no answer to this, except for a curt, 'Drink?'

'A vodka and tonic, please. Yet you took Lucy and Pauline to London with you, didn't you?'

'Yes.'

'Do you often take them both with you?'

Jennifer fully expected him to tell her to mind her own business but instead she said, 'No but I wanted Lucy to see a particular doctor that I know.'

'Is something wrong with her?' Jennifer exclaimed in alarm.

'No.' He gave an odd little smile. 'And that's all I'm saying upon the subject, Jennifer.'

And, as was beginning to happen every time he said her name, a strange little shiver travelled along Jennifer's spine.

# Seven

An uneasy silence lay between Jennifer and Jake then and, in spite of her surprise to see her, Jennifer was almost relieved when Pauline Duvall rejoined them in the lounge prior to dinner. Pauline had changed out of her working clothes and into a low-cut, sapphire-blue, clinging silk affair.

Pauline must have discerned Jennifer's astonishment because, she said in answer to Jake's, 'Drink, Pauline?' 'My usual dry sherry, please,' and then, and this was said directly to Jennifer, 'I've had the last few evenings free, Miss Bell, if you're wondering why I haven't been in the habit of joining you both. They were owing to me. When we're both in, then we dine together. Isn't that right, Jake?'

So, mused Jennifer, it was the custom for Pauline to dine with Jake, was it? Had she joined Esther and Jake in the same manner before Esther's suicide?

Jake said nothing. He had his back to the two women and was busy at the tray of drinks pouring Pauline her dry sherry. Nonetheless, Jennifer would have given the earth for a glimpse of his expression.

'How long are you planning to stay with us, Miss Bell?' Pauline suddenly asked, as with a slanting smile up at Jake she took her drink.

'For three or four weeks, at least.' Jake took it upon himself to answer for Jennifer. His gaze measured her startled glance up at him, daring her to argue with him, it seemed. 'I'd like to get to know Jennifer properly and allow her to know – us.' His pause seemed to imply that what he had wanted to say was 'me' but that at the last minute he had thought better of it.

Pauline appeared decidedly displeased by this and her eyes were cool as she asked, 'But surely – your newspaper awaits your return?'

'As I'm here on an assignment for my paper, Miss Duvall, my editor will quite understand why when I don't return immediately.'

Which, by the glint of satisfaction that appeared within Jake's eyes, undoubtedly bestowed the impression that she was perfectly happy to remain at Peacock House for the length of time that he had laid down. As that hadn't been the impression that she had intended conveying at all, Jennifer realized that she had unwittingly talked herself into a rather tight corner. Her lips tightened in annoyance with herself.

'And what assignment would that be?' Pauline then went to ask.

'A follow-up feature on Esther. What effect her death has had on her family, the local community, her friends . . . .'

Pauline grimaced. 'How perfectly gruesome.'

'Yes, that was my initial opinion when my editor first put the suggestion to me, but then, I began to see it as a way of paying our respects to the wife of a prominent businessman and well-known novelist. I plan to present it in the form of a written memorial to Esther.'

'How quaint.' Pauline's eyes signalled her hostility to the whole thing as she slowly sipped at her sherry.

But Jake's eyes were gleaming, ironic amusement filling them as he remarked, somewhat drily, 'I didn't know I was so well thought of in media circles.

'Jennifer and Esther were once friends,' he then went on.

'Yes I know,' Pauline replied. 'Lucy told me.'

Dinner proved a tense affair after that, with Pauline gibing at Jennifer at every opportunity. Jake simply reclined into his seat, making no attempt to participate. In fact, the whole thing seemed to be providing him with some sort of perverted amusement, Jennifer concluded.

Dinner was over and they were drinking their coffee when a tiny voice spoke from the doorway. 'Daddy.'

It was Lucy, clutching her teddy bear and rubbing her eyes.

She looked utterly adorable and Jennifer felt her heart go out to the motherless child. Esther might not have been the world's most perfect mother but she was – had been – the only one that this little girl had had. Pauline Duvall was certainly no substitute. Even if she hoped to be some time in the future.

'Lucy – what is it?' Jake's voice was tense – almost as if he were trying very hard to hold on to his temper.

Once again, Jennifer felt angry with him. How could

he even consider putting someone like Pauline in Esther's place? The woman had no affection for Lucy; that was only too obvious from thc manner in which she regarded the child now. Intense irritation glittered within her eyes as her lips thinned into a tight, uncompromising line.

'I want a drink. Pauline wouldn't let me have one. . . .' Lucy glowered at her nurse and Jennifer found herself biting back a chuckle of amusement.

'Lucy,' Pauline's voice was sharp with her irritation, 'that's not true.'

Jake was watching his daughter so he didn't see the expression that arrived in the nurse's eye as she looked at Lucy. But Jennifer saw it and it made her distinctly uneasy. A hard glint conveyed actual dislike of her small charge.

'Go back to bed, Lucy. Pauline will bring you up some water, I promise.' Jake's tone betrayed an unexpected indulgence with the small girl. Perhaps he wasn't as indifferent to Lucy as he appeared, Jennifer mused. She was his child after all.

But Lucy wasn't having any of it.

'I want you to bring it, Daddy – please,' she ended on a pleading note.

'All right.' Again Jake did the unexpected.

Jennifer suddenly had the notion that maybe her words earlier had had some effect upon him. Stranger things had happened.

'And Jennifer,' Lucy added, mischievously.

'Lucy,' Pauline began, her tone far sharper than the situation warranted, 'you can't expect a guest . . . .'

Jake interrupted. 'Jennifer?'

Jennifer looked away from Pauline and straight at

him. 'Yes?'

'Do you mind?' Dark eyes glittered at her, expectantly, challengingly almost . . . .

'No, not at all.'

'Go back to bed, Lucy.' Amusement definitely shone from the black eyes now. 'You've won.'

Lucy skipped away, obviously completely content now that her demands had been met.

'We won't need you any more this evening, Pauline.'

It was dismissal. Pauline knew it; Jennifer knew it.

The woman's top lip curled but she didn't speak. She simply stood up, replacing her napkin carefully on to the table, and walked across the room. Jennifer felt a reluctant admiration for her. She wondered if she would have behaved so well under similar circumstances. Because she was as certain as she could be, without positive proof, that something had gone on between Jake and his daughter's nurse, even if it wasn't still happening.

Jake strode into the kitchen, fetching Lucy's drink while Jennifer waited at the foot of the stairs. Of Pauline there was no sign. She must have gone to her room.

When they got to Lucy's room, the little girl was sitting up in bed, surrounded by a mass of soft toys.

'My, my!' Jennifer exclaimed. 'Won't you introduce me to your friends, Lucy?'

Lucy gurgled with laughter and patted the space to one side of the pillow. 'You sit here, Jennifer.'

Jennifer did as she was told.

Whereupon Lucy promptly patted her other side, saying smugly, 'There's room for you here, Daddy.'

Jake grinning at a vastly amused Jennifer also did as

he was bidden.

Lucy snuggled down between them, emitting a very satisfied sigh. 'Now we're a family.'

A movement in the open doorway made all three of them look up. Pauline stood there.

'Well, how cosy,' she sneered.

'Go away, Pauline,' Lucy retorted, sitting up once more. 'We don't need you.'

'Really. Why don't you ask your daddy about that, Lucy?' Her smile at Jake was pure malice.

Jennifer couldn't resist darting a sideways glance at Jake; his expression revealed nothing, however.

'Can you spare me a moment, Jake?' From the way Pauline spoke it was quite clear, to Jennifer at least, that the words weren't meant as a request; they were definitely a command.

It was evident that Jake discerned the same thing because his tone was curt as he asked, 'Can't it wait, Pauline?'

'No.' Pauline spoke every bit as abruptly, before turning and stalking away.

'It's all right, Daddy,' Lucy spoke up, 'you can go. Jennifer will read me a story.'

Jennifer didn't quite bite back her hysterical laugh at hearing Jake so summarily dismissed by his adorable five-year-old daughter. But her involuntary glance up at Jake soon dispelled the urge to laugh. His gaze all but froze her right where she sat.

Lucy pulled at Jennifer's arm and somehow she managed to smile at the child, as if none of it mattered – which, of course, it did, desperately. So, as a consequence, she didn't see Jake leave the room.

'There's the book, Jennifer, on the chair. It's my

favourite.'

Somehow Jennifer managed to concentrate her mind sufficiently to read the book right through, only stumbling once or twice when she found she couldn't quite banish the images that invaded her mind. By the time she had finished, Lucy was fast asleep, teddy bear clutched to her breast and her thumb firmly encapsulated by her rosebud mouth. Slowly Jennifer replaced the book upon the chair and tucking the blankets more securely round Lucy, she bent and deposited a kiss upon the satin-smooth cheek. Lucy didn't stir.

Quietly, Jennifer walked from the room and began to move towards her own bedroom. It was then that she heard the sounds of voices. They were coming from downstairs, from the lounge.

Although she couldn't distinguish any words – the door was firmly closed – it was perfectly clear from their tones that Jake and Pauline were arguing. Jennifer lingered on the landing for a moment, unable to help herself, straining to hear what was being said, until, ashamed of herself for this exhibition of blatant eavesdropping, she ran to her own room.

Jennifer walked into the village for her meeting with Chris on the following evening. True to her word, she hadn't told Jake who she was having dinner with, simply excusing herself from the evening meal and not deigning to give a reason.

The chances were that he wouldn't miss her presence anyway – not with Pauline to divert him. It had been Lucy who had appeared most disturbed by her threatened absence. Jennifer had given way to the child's blandishments and read her a story once Lucy had been lured into bed and then, of course, it had been a mad rush to prepare herself for her dinner date.

Date? Was that what it was? she wondered as she walked along between the high hedgerows that lined the lane leading from Peacock House into Trezillian and the Smuggler's Arms. No, she'd think of it as another interview for now. She refused to become involved with another man – not while David was still in her life – not even one as attractive as Chris Williams. She firmly pushed the thoughts of Jake Richardson to one side. She fully intended to enjoy herself this evening.

A skylark sang overhead as she walked along. The high hedgerows were a rich, luxuriant green, interspersed with daisies, the odd wild rose and the frothy heads of the ubiquitous cow parsley. She breathed in the scented air, forgetting, for the moment, the discord that prevailed during the previous evening at Peacock House. In the distance she could hear the boom of the waves as they struck the town quay.

Jennifer had dressed for this evening in lightweight cream linen trousers and a high-necked, long-sleeved, olive-green blouse. As demure as the blouse seemed, the soft fabric somehow managed to accentuate the small, high breasts, bestowing a tantalizing impression of mystery and promise. Not that Jennifer realized this, just as she hadn't realized what a perfect foil the colour was for her chestnut hair and brilliant green eyes. The warm sea breezes had already tanned her creamy complexion to an alluring gold, thus enhancing even further the colour of her hair and eyes. With her slender, almost boyish, figure and her long, shapely legs she presented a picture that most men would find totally irresistable. And Chris Williams proved no exception.

'Wow!' he enthused as he stood to greet her in the small lounge bar of the hotel. 'I'm going to have every other man here tonight green with envy.'

And as modest as she was, Jennifer did have to admit that when they took their seats in the restaurant, she was indeed the target for every eye in the place, male and female. The knowledge wasn't entirely unwelcome. Her ego, sorely battered after the previous evening's conclusion, stood in desperate need of a boost.

It wasn't until she saw Jake stride in with two other men and met the glare that came her way when he saw whom she was with, that she began to feel uncomfortable. Although why she felt that way she couldn't have said. Jake had no rights over her, after all. It didn't help to see that Chris was every bit as uncomfortable. He kept shooting glances across at Jake as if fearful of what the other man would do. But what could Jake do? Nothing, she repeatedly told herself.

They were halfway through their meal when events took a dramatic and unforeseen twist. And Jennifer wished herself anywhere but sitting in The Smuggler's Arms, directly under Jake Richardson's sardonic gaze.

She was lifting a forkful of delicious crab salad to her lips when a low, but obviously furious, voice said, 'So this is where you are, you – you rotter. You didn't think I'd come back early, did you? Who is she? Answer me that. Who are you, you bitch? That's my husband you're with.' And with that, the woman leant forward and slapped Jennifer straight across the face.

# Eight

Jennifer raised a trembling hand to her smarting cheek, staring wide-eyed at the woman standing over with her hand raised for a second slap.

'Jilly!' Chris leapt to his feet, only just in time to prevent the woman who claimed to be his wife from taking another swing at Jennifer. 'It isn't what you think.'

But Jilly Williams was in no mood to listen. 'Oh, isn't it? Then tell me just what it is?'

'Please, Mrs Williams,' Jennifer began. 'I'm a journalist. I'm here simply to conduct an interview with your husband.'

'Oh, save it,' Jilly sneered. 'I don't believe a word of it in any case.' She tugged her arm free of her husband's grip.

'Jilly,' Chris tried again, 'sweetheart . . . .'

'Don't you sweetheart me, you – you . . . .'

'Jennifer.'

The rich, dark brown voice broke in, restoring some semblance of normality to a situation that was fast degenerating into a farce. Jennifer glanced up and couldn't hide her relief at seeing Jake standing there – right behind Jilly Williams. He had a restraining hand upon the arm that was once more raised in anger.

'Jilly, you've got this all wrong. Jennifer has only just arrived in Trezillian and as she says she is a journalist.'

Jilly seemed to weigh up Jake's words and noticeably calmed down. 'Oh I see. Well maybe I have misunderstood . . . this time.' She glowered at her husband again.

Chris glanced about the room at the sea of staring faces, every eye was riveted upon them. His fair skin flushed with his embarrassment. 'I would hardly have brought Jennifer here, where everyone knows me, if there'd been something clandestine about it.' He spoke now in a low voice as he caught hold of his raging wife. 'Just let me explain.'

'Get your hands off me,' Jilly commanded him from between clenched teeth. 'That's the very thing you would do – bring her here. Just to throw me off the scent . . . .'

Jennifer slid her glance across to Jake. Upon seeing his sideways flick of the head, she understood at once what he was indicating. Leave husband and wife to argue it out between themselves. She promptly stood up and, with as much dignity as she could muster, began to walk from the room. If every eye hadn't been glued to her upon her entrance, it certainly was upon her exit. Her colour was high as she left the restaurant. Jake followed her.

Once they were outside, he turned her to face him. He assessed the sheen of tears within her eyes, the imprints of Jilly's fingers still emblazoned on her skin. Then he lifted a hand and gently touched the reddened marks. 'It doesn't take you long to stir emotions, does it?' His voice was husky and for a second she wondered whose emotions precisely he was referring to?

The dark eyes smouldered down at her. 'Is this your usual way of doing things?'

And, with a jolt, she realized that the emotion that she could see within him was fury.

'I don't know what you mean.'

'Don't you? Did you know you were meeting a married man?'

'Actually, no, I didn't.'

'Well – a word of warning, Jennifer –' As invariably happened when he spoke her name, a shiver of delight rippled through Jennifer. 'Chris Williams is an inveterate womanizer. His wife clearly knows it too. Stay away from him. Jilly has had enough to put up with over the years without you adding to her unhappiness.'

Jennifer blinked up at him That was rich. Him telling her to stay away from a man, actually sympathizing with the deceived wife. When, from the evidence of last night, it looked as if he'd been doing the very same thing himself.

'Is that the pot calling the kettle black?' she waspishly asked.

His eyes narrowed at her. 'What does that rather barbed little comment mean?'

'As if you didn't know?'

'No, I'm afraid I don't know. You'll have to enlighten me.'

'I heard you and Pauline last night – in the lounge.'

'Aah.'

'There's something going on between you, isn't there? Was it going on while Esther was alive?'

'Jennifer . . . .' he paused, as if searching for the right words.

'So, I'm right,' she sneered. 'You hypocrite! You condemn Chris Williams for doing the very thing that you're doing.'

'Jennifer,' Jake said again, 'there's nothing going on between Pauline and I . . . .'

'Hah!' she exclaimed hotly. 'That wasn't what the rumours and gossip said six months ago. Something must have fuelled all the speculation of an affair between you and Pauline. After all, you did take her to London and stay overnight with her.'

He arched an eyebrow at her tone.

'You don't want to believe all the papers say. I'd have thought you'd have known that, Jennifer, being a member of that disreputable fraternity yourself.' His tone was biting and full of contempt as he went on. 'But then that's what your lot thrive on, isn't it? Gossip, rumour, speculation . . . you'd all go bankrupt without it. If you can't find something salacious enough to print, you simply make it up. Is that what you're really here for? To dig up any dirt that might have been missed the first time round?'

He had moved closer without Jennifer noticing and now they were practically nose to nose, glaring at each other through the darkness. 'Although, I have to admit – fool that I am – I had begun to hope that you were the exception.'

He lifted both hands and grasped her by the arms. It was the first time he had touched her and the impact of his fingers upon her produced a shockwave the like of which Jennifer had never before experienced. She suppressed a groan.

'No. Please,' she protested weakly.

He shook her roughly. 'Please what?' His tone, as well as his expression now, was subtly mocking, which, not surprisingly, went a long way toward resurrecting Jennifer's fury at him.

She decided to disregard his accusations of her real purpose in coming to Trezillian. They were too close to the mark for her to be able to deny them with any sincerity. Instead, she demanded, 'Was there any truth in the reported rumours, Jake? Was that why Esther killed herself?' She shook herself free of his punishing grip. 'Because you were somewhere else with your mistress while she was at home, alone and pregnant?'

She was taunting him, she freely acknowledged, to the point that, for a second, she thought she'd well and truly overstepped the mark and he was going to hit her. His face hardened until it resembled granite rather than mere flesh, and she saw a small muscle begin to flex in his cheek. His eyes had darkened until they were the exact shade of ebony and when he spoke his voice was cold and implacable. 'There was some truth, yes – in the reports of an affair. But what the papers didn't realize, and you clearly haven't either, is that the affair that was going on wasn't mine; it was Esther's. And it wasn't the first – not by a long chalk.'

'Esther's,' Jennifer breathed. So – she'd been right when she'd suddenly wondered if that was the way it had been.

'Yes. And, as I said, it wasn't the first. She'd indulged in them regularly over the last four or five years. She was here' – he indicated the hotel – 'on the night of her death to meet a man. I'm convinced of that.'

Jake suddenly reached for her and pulled her into his arms. 'In which case,' he muttered throatily, 'I think I'm entitled to take my own small moment of pleasure. . . don't you?' His head bent to hers. And although his lids lowered over his eyes, they didn't close completely, so Jennifer found herself staring, as if mesmerized, into the narrowed, liquid depths. The kiss that ensued was a revelation – and not just for her, Jennifer suspected. After their mouths had clung for several moments, Jake pulled back, staring at her. He was obviously shaken but even so, Jennifer couldn't tell what he was thinking. But then, she quizzed herself sardonically, when had she ever been able to? She'd never seen anyone shutter his expression so totally as Jake Richardson before. Very, very slowly, Jake lowered his head to hers again and although she knew she should be running for her life, this time, Jennifer couldn't prevent herself from responding as she had never before responded to any man. She was experiencing the sort of reaction that till now she'd only ever either read about, or written about in her own novels. Her body felt as if it were on fire, her blood sang, joyously, as it sped through her veins, her heart thundered so loudly it was amazing that Jake didn't hear it, and her pulses throbbed fit to burst. She wanted him. God help her; she loved him.

Marshalling every one of her broken defences, Jennifer finally wrenched herself free. He mustn't be allowed to guess at the truth. If he knew that she loved him, she couldn't possibly stay at Peacock House.

'How dare you?' she cried.

'Oh, for goodness sake,' was Jake's unmoved response to that. 'Spare me the maidenly modesty, it's not your style. . . .'

She lifted a hand and slapped him, straight across the cheek. He made no move to retaliate. Just his eyes glittered at her. Then, as she dropped her hand to her side again, desperately ashamed of her loss of control, he simply said, 'If you ever do that again, my girl, you'll live to regret it. Take my word for it.' He turned away from her then, rasping out, 'I'll drive you home.'

'You will not. I'll walk,' was her frosty reply. Not for anything would she sit alongside him – not even for the relatively short ride back to the house. Her cheeks were burning with embarrassment at her behaviour of the past few moments. What had she been thinking of? First, she'd kissed him with a passion she hadn't dreamt she was capable of – and let's face it, she scathingly and silently told herself, Jake Richardson was more than man enough to recognize passion when he was on the receiving end of it – then, she'd had the sheer effrontery to slap him. Whatever must he be thinking of her?

'Get into the car, Jennifer.'

She met his implacable gaze, defiance registering in every stiff line of her.

'Do you want me to pick you up and put you in myself? Because, rest assured, I will.' Something, it could have been amusement, flickered at her from his face as he spoke and Jennifer realized with that how foolish she was being. Did she really wish to walk along that inky lane, alone, at this time of night? No, of course she didn't.

Having no option but to recognize abject defeat when it stared her in the face, therefore, she did as he bade and meekly climbed into the car that was parked immediately in front of the small hotel. She had to give him his due, he made no show of crowing his triumph over her. Instead, he drove back to Peacock House, the silence between them absolute.

However, things weren't over between them, not by any means. When Jennifer walked down to the breakfast-room next morning, determined to tell Jake that she was leaving that day, he was waiting for her, a half-empty cup of coffee in front of him.

He folded up the newspaper that he had clearly been reading and, looking up at her as she walked into the room, said with characteristic forthrightness, 'I think we need to talk, Jennifer. A few things need clearing up between us.'

'Really, and what things would they be?' Her tone was waspish.

Jake seemed not to notice. 'Things like my relationship with Esther, with Pauline and not least, Lucy.'

'Ah yes, Lucy,' Jennifer bit out. 'Poor, unwanted little Lucy.'

'Will you just wait to hear what I have to say before you accuse, try and pass sentence?' he finally lashed back. 'My God, you do take a lot upon yourself, don't you, with your blasted assumptions?'

Jennifer fell silent.

'Thank you,' he said, with exaggerated politeness.

'Esther and I haven't had a marriage in the true sense of the word for at least four years. Since just after Lucy was born, in fact. Her affairs, as I told you last night, were numerous and fairly well known.'

'But – surely,' Jennifer began haltingly, 'you must bear some of the blame for that. A happy, fulfilled woman doesn't indulge in affairs. Even you must admit that.'

'I agree,' he replied mildly. 'The trouble was – as I told you a few days ago – to keep Esther happy and fulfilled,' he sarcastically echoed her words, 'I needed to dance attendance upon her all day, every day. I didn't have the time, or in the latter years,' he amended bitterly, 'the inclination. I had books to write, supermarkets to oversee, especially in the early days when I was building up the chain. If Esther were to have the luxurious style of life that she demanded then I needed to put in the hours. She couldn't, or wouldn't, see that. So, when I failed to live up to her high and, frankly, impossible expectations, she turned elsewhere for the attention that I hadn't given her. The birth of Lucy was a responsibility that she didn't want and certainly hadn't planned for – whatever she might have told you to the contrary. She hated being tied by a small, constantly demanding child so she hired a nurse and that was that – which brings me to Pauline.'

Jennifer didn't say anything. By the manner in which Jake frowned at her, she suspected her facial expression said it all for her.

'I admit there was something between Pauline and I . . .'

'I knew it,' Jennifer muttered under her breath.

'. . . but not until after Esther had – gone. I'm only human, after all, and I was at a very low ebb. Suffice it to say, that momentary weakness proved to be the biggest mistake of my life. It gave Pauline expectations of better things.'

'All these women and their tiresome expectations,' Jennifer gibed.

Jake disregarded that completely, other than for a grim tightening of his mouth, and continued, 'Which I have no intention of allowing her, It was wrong of me, I admit, but as God is my witness, Jennifer,' his voice deepened as he stared at her, 'it only happened once. It didn't take me long to realize what I had done; what I had led her to hope for.' He shrugged hopelessly. 'Since then she's tried everything to get me back into her bed.'

'What it is to be irresistible!'

Jake appraised her from beneath lowered eyelids. 'And having failed is becoming increasingly bitter. Hence, the row that you overheard.'

'I see.'

'It won't be happening again, you have my word on that.'

'It really isn't any of my business,' she said in a deliberately off-hand manner. 'But – how can you be so sure of that, Jake?' she couldn't resist asking.

Jake stared at her for a minute and then said in a low voice, 'Oh, I can be. Take it from me. Pauline's gone.'

'Gone? Gone where?' Jennifer looked at him, her astonishment plain to see.

He shrugged. 'I haven't the foggiest idea. She left last night – while you were out.'

Jennifer carefully weighed him up. 'Did you sack her?'

'Let's call it a mutually arrived at decision.'

'You sacked her,' she declared bluntly. 'Who's going

to look after Lucy now?'

'I will – with the assistance of Mrs Elliot.'

'Don't you mean Mrs Elliott will?' Jennifer demanded heatedly, disproportionately irritated by his high-handed attitude towards the various women in his life. 'Hasn't that poor woman got enough to do already? Without having to look after a child too? She's not getting any younger, you know.'

'Will you calm down?' Jake appeared only amused at her fierce response to his words when really, when all was said and done, it was nothing to do with her. Within a day or two, if she had her way, she would be gone – if not sooner, she mused ironically. In fact, he might be working up to telling her to leave as well – to stop her interfering any further in his life. 'Don't you get yourself worked up over nothing?' he now went on.

Jennifer tightened her lips at him. 'I don't regard Lucy as nothing. She's already suffering from a chronic lack of affection upon your part. The child is emotionally neglected, that's what's wrong with her.'

Jake's expression warned her that, this time, she'd gone too far.

But then, unable to resist the temptation to show him that her criticism was fully justified she went on, 'Do you know what Lucy said to me the first time we met? Shall I tell you?'

'You might as well,' Jake rather wearily agreed, 'I'm sure that nothing I can say will stop you.'

'"My daddy doesn't like me",' Jennifer burst out. 'That's what the child said.'

She saw Jake flinch at that.

'I think there's something else I ought to tell you, Jennifer.'

'I'm sure there is,' she smartly retaliated, her ire well and truly raised by now.

'I don't think Lucy is my child.'

# Nine

If Jake had slapped her, Jennifer couldn't have displayed more amazement than she did in the aftermath of that blunt declaration.

'What?' she cried.

'That's what I took Lucy to London for, the night that Esther took the overdose. To have blood tests done. For possible proof of paternity. The only trouble with a blood test is – it can prove quite definitely that I'm not the father but not positively that I am.'

'And?'

'I could be. That's all they could tell me.'

'You're mad! What's made you doubt that Lucy's yours?'

'Esther.' He smiled grimly. 'She told me Lucy wasn't mine during one particularly nasty row. It was about twelve months before she died – I'd adored Lucy till then.' His harsh features softened momentarily. 'If Esther had stuck a knife into me she couldn't have wounded me more. Every time I look at Lucy now I wonder . . . . Anyway, I finally decided I had to know – one way or the other. So that's where we were. Obviously if I had had the slightest suspicion of Esther's intentions I wouldn't have gone . . . .'

'But why haven't you had DNA testing?' Jennifer burst out. 'That would tell you positively.'

'Yes, I know. They recommended that when they couldn't confirm that she was really mine. But when it came to the crunch – of finding out without a shadow of doubt – well, I didn't have the courage then, and I don't have it now. What if they show she's not mine? What do I do then? Especially now that Esther's . . . . I decided to leave matters as they stood.'

'But – of course Lucy's yours,' Jennifer exclaimed. 'There's no mistaking the resemblance. Oh,' she shook her head at his sceptical expression, 'she doesn't look much like you, I know, but her mannerisms, the way she has of tossing her head, the quirk of her eyebrows, her very way of talking – they're all you, Jake. There's no mistaking that you're her father.

'Is that why you're so uncaring of Lucy?'

He lifted an eyebrow at her. She laughed out aloud. It was Lucy looking at her.

'I wasn't aware that I was,' he retorted stiffly.

'Only sometimes. But as I said – Lucy's noticed it.'

'I'll have to try harder then.'

'Jake?' Jennifer suddenly decided to confide her doubts to him.

'Mmmm?'

'Had you wondered . . . well, if Esther had gone to meet a man that last night? That he might have been the one to contribute towards her suicide? Rather than the state of your marriage as all the papers suggested at the time.'

'Yes,' Jake was frowning. 'But with no proof of anyone having met her there . . . .' He shrugged his shoulders.

'Did you say anything to the police about your suspicions?'

'No. What would have been the point? It would have just supplied the papers with even more reason to speculate and gossip and I considered there'd already been enough of that. Esther killed herself for – whatever reason. Let her rest in peace now. God knows, she must have been unhappy enough in her last few weeks.' For the first time then, Jennifer saw sorrow upon Jake's face. 'I failed her so she turned elsewhere for comfort – and love . . . I can't blame her.'

'No, Jake.' The look upon his face tore at Jennifer. 'You didn't fail her. She failed herself in the end. Esther always went for the easy option – even as a small girl. You mustn't blame yourself.'

A few days later, Jake asked Jennifer out to dinner. Jennifer had decided to stay at Peacock House for just a while longer. Not even to herself would she admit that it wasn't only her work responsible for that decision. She'd spoken to a few more people about Esther but other than for politely expressed regrets at her death, she learnt no more than she'd known before. She was still no nearer to finding out the real reason for Esther's suicide. If only she'd left a note . . . . It certainly hadn't been because of infidelity on the part of Jake – as the newspapers at the time had hinted. Jake, by his own words, had made a nonsense of that theory – and

Jennifer believed him.

'Dress up,' Jake commanded. 'It's Saturday night; we'll go somewhere special.'

So that's what they did.

Jennifer selected her most flattering dress to wear, a pale-green fitted sheath that brought out the colour of her eyes as well as the rich tones of her hair. Its smooth, uncluttered lines also made the most of her slender curves, showing off to the best advantage possible the long, sleek legs and slender, finely boned ankles. She wanted this evening to be one that both Jake and she would look back on with pleasure. And Jake's eyes, when she descended into the hallway where he was waiting for her, told her all that she needed to know. Nonetheless, it was extremely gratifying to have this confirmed in actual words.

'You look lovely.'

'So do you!' she chipped back in a lighthearted attempt to conceal the wild surge of pleasure that his words induced. And, indeed, he did look splendid. His tall, powerful frame was clothed entirely in black and white; black jacket and trousers, brilliant white shirt. It emphasized his dark, good looks as well as his magnificent physique. Jennifer felt a shiver of anticipation ripple through her. Would he kiss her again? She realized in that second just how much she wanted him to.

Lucy had been allowed to wait up and wave them off and she did so now, her innocent words endorsing her father's compliment.

'You look bewtiful, Jennifer,' she whispered.

'Thank you, darling.' Jennifer kissed her peach-like cheek. 'I'll see you tomorrow.'

Relations had improved dramatically between Jake

and Lucy. Since Jennifer had reassured him of her belief in his paternity, he'd lavished love and affection upon his small daughter, as if trying desperately to make up for the harm that his wilful wife had caused. Lucy blossomed beneath his attentions. She no longer resorted to tantrums to get her own way. She didn't need to. A flick of her long eyelashes and her father responded with all the love that he was capable of, tenderly giving way to her smallest demand. Jennifer had wondered at one point if Esther had been jealous of Jake's love for his small daughter and so had set out to destroy and corrupt it. If that had been her intention, she had almost succeeded. She was slowly realizing that Esther had changed dramatically since she had known her.

'Be a good girl, poppet,' Jake now said, 'and go to bed when Mrs Elliot tells you.'

''Night, 'night, Daddy.' She held her arms up for him to lift her and drop a kiss upon her cheek. She wrapped her arms about his neck, widening her eyes at Jennifer over his shoulder as she did so. 'I wish you would be my new mummy, Jennifer.'

Jennifer felt the hot rush of colour into her face, Jake didn't respond despite Lucy's crafty, sideways glance. The little imp, thought Jennifer in some amusement, she'd known exactly what she was doing then.

'Goodnight, Lucy,' she managed to say, before turning towards the door, in a frantic attempt to hide her hot cheeks before Jake turned and saw them. Lord knows what he would make of her embarrassment. Most likely leap to the only conclusion he could. That she longed for the same thing that Lucy did.

'You'll still be here tomorrow, won't you?' Lucy added.

'Yes, of course I will. I won't go without saying goodbye to you. But I'll really have to leave in a day or two, poppet,' she warned. 'I've got a job to get back to.'

'Daddy, make her stay with us. I don't want her to go.' Lucy's bright blue eyes filled with what seemed genuine tears.

'Now, now, Lucy,' Jake stood her on the floor again. 'You leave that to Jennifer and me to sort out.'

Jennifer glanced at him, startled by what he had said. Surely he didn't mean . . . ? No, she was imagining things.

Jake said nothing more upon the subject so she decided that he had said what he'd said simply to placate his small daughter. He took Jennifer to a very expensive country hotel just outside of Newquay, on the north coast of Cornwall. They ate superbly prepared food and then danced to an orchestra that played all of Jennifer's favourite tunes. It was a perfect evening and Jennifer knew that she was falling deeper in love with Jake with every moment that passed.

Jake held her close as they danced and all of a sudden, she felt his lips in her hair. Her body curved of its own volition into his and she sighed as he gathered her closer. If only . . . .

As she'd said to Lucy, her work here was all but concluded. She couldn't delay her departure much longer, no matter how deeply she yearned to. She'd found out all she was going to be able to, she suspected, about the circumstances surrounding Esther's death. As the coroner had concluded at the inquest, "Suicide while the balance of the mind was disturbed". There was nothing else she intended saying about it. She would tell Bill that she'd found nothing worth printing about either Jake or Esther. That, in her opinion, they'd led blameless existences. He would take her word for it. She felt a fleeting spasm of guilt at her deception but she swiftly smothered it. Nothing had happened to change her conviction that her first loyalty in all of this lay with Esther and nothing in the world would persuade her to splash Esther's infidelities all over the front pages of the *Chronicle*. Because she had no doubt that that's precisely where they would end up.

There was just one thing that she still needed to ask Jake, that she personally needed to know, and she resolved to put the question to him tonight, over dinner.

They'd eaten their meal and were enjoying a coffee and a brandy when Jennifer suddenly asked, 'There's just one thing I'd like to ask you, Jake.'

'Fire away,' he invited, his gaze warm as it lingered appreciatively upon her bright eyes and slightly flushed cheeks. 'You really have the most delightful habit of blushing, Jennifer Bell,' he murmured. 'I thought today's woman had forgotten how.'

His remark threw Jennifer. It wasn't what she'd been expecting. Jake Richardson seemed to have the ability to disconcert her at a moment's notice. It was disturbing. Nonetheless, she tried to disregard his slow smile as he watched her blush deepen and his almost indiscernible, 'See what I mean? Gorgeous!' to ask him, 'Esther was pregnant at the time of her suicide. Was it your baby or her most recent lover's?'

'Aah. I wondered when you'd get round to that,' he murmured. His one finger began to tap on the table top as he continued to contemplate her. Finally, he said, 'It could have been mine.'

Jennifer tried, she really did, but she couldn't conceal her dismay at his answer. 'But – but I thought you said the marriage was over . . . .?'

His gaze measured her, absorbing the green eyes that were now shadowed, the full lips that turned down just slightly at the corners as she met his look. 'Jennifer . . . .' He put out a hand and caught one of hers that were lying on the table top. 'It was – it was a . . . .' he paused, as if searching for the appropriate words, 'a one-off occasion. The sort that happens when you've both had one drink too many and . . .' he glanced down at her slender fingers, holding so tightly on to his now, 'I'm only human after all. Esther was still a beautiful woman, no matter what I thought of her morals. I was – am – still a man with normal needs and desires. So, I suppose technically, yes, it could have been mine. Personally, and as it was the first time that we had shared a bed in over three years, I think it was much more likely to have been the current lover's. But,' he shrugged, 'who could say?'

'Jake, do you know who the other man was?'

'No. And I don't want to either. So if you know who it was, please don't tell me.'

That sounded as if he still cared about Esther, Jennifer thought miserably. 'No, I don't know. But why should she kill herself, knowing she was pregnant? I don't understand it.'

'Perhaps she didn't know, not for certain.'

'Perhaps not. But why kill herself at all? What made her do it, Jake? I've tried to tell myself the coroner was right and it was while the balance of her mind was disturbed. It doesn't ring true. Oh, I know the doctor said she was depressed but depressed enough to take her own life? Wouldn't you have noticed?'

'Possibly not, Jennifer. Despite that last time that we shared a bed, we each led our own lives. I didn't see that much of her. She was always out somewhere or other.'

'Janey Wilson, when I spoke to her, said that Esther had changed in her last few weeks. Did you think that?'

Jake looked thoughtful. 'I don't think her affairs brought Esther happiness, certainly. In the end, I think they might have killed her. If you want the blunt truth, I think Esther had lost her self-respect.'

All too soon the evening was over. They walked, side by side, to the car. Being two of the last dinner-dance guests to arrive they'd been forced to park on the far side of the extensive car-park – beneath some tall chestnut trees.

They'd almost reached the car when Jennifer, unused to wearing high-heeled shoes, stumbled upon the uneven ground, and lurched forward. Jake's arm shot out, catching her by the elbow the exact moment before she would have sunk to her knees; he held her steady while she regained her balance.

Jennifer turned her head to thank him and was stopped from saying anything at all by the expression that blazed from his face at her.

'Jennifer. . . .' he muttered, pulling her in to his side.

Thoroughly shaken by what she'd seen upon Jake's face, Jennifer slid an arm about his waist, more for support than anything else, but it quickly became obvious that Jake had other ideas. He quickened his pace, drawing her in beneath the thick canopy of chestnut foliage as he did so. He swung her then, positioning her between the tree trunk and his own body, thereby concealing her from any chance passer-by. His arm remained about her waist. Jennifer looked up at him, her breath catching in her throat once more at what she saw.

Black eyes, heavy lidded and irradiated with gold flecks, glinted through the night at her. They stared at each other for an endless moment before Jake slowly lowered his face to hers. He didn't kiss her straight away. Instead, he brought out his tongue and very, very gently ran its tip over her parted lips – as if he were tasting her, relishing her sweetness.

'Oh God, Jennifer,' he suddenly groaned, pulling her closer and sliding his other arm about her too. 'I can't help myself. Since that last time . . . you're so lovely, I can't resist this . . . .' And so saying, he closed the tiny gap between their mouths, almost instantly increasing the pressure of his, till he seemed to be all but possessing her, capturing the very essence of her, and all Jennifer could do was respond, blindly and with everything that was in her . . . .

# Ten

As if trying to make her last days at Peacock House a special time for them all, the following day, Jake asked Lucy and Jennifer, 'Who fancies a drive out this afternoon for a picnic?' Lucy immediately clapped her small hands together, gazing expectantly at Jennifer as she answered, 'Oh, Daddy, what a fab'lus idea.'

'Jennifer?' Jake then asked, the expectancy contained within his dark eyes an exact imitation of his daughter's expression.

'That sounds like a good idea,' Jennifer smiled at them both.

'Good. I'll go tell Mrs Elliot to pack us a hamper then and we'll be off.'

An hour later, they were sitting in Jake's luxurious Jaguar, Jennifer in the front passenger seat and Lucy securely strapped into the rear, her favourite doll sitting at her side and her favourite picture book upon her knee. The picnic hamper was in the boot.

'Where are we going, Daddy?'

'I thought Dartmoor. Maybe we'll be lucky enough to catch a glimpse of the wild ponies. What do you think, Lucy?'

'Have you ever seen the ponies, Jennifer?' Lucy asked.

'No, I've never been to Dartmoor so it will be a first-time experience for me on both counts, Lucy.'

The drive to Devon and on to Dartmoor was a journey well worth taking for Jennifer. Not only did she get to sit close to Jake for a satisfyingly long period of time, but she also got to see some pretty spectacular scenery. Greedily, she feasted her eyes upon the flower-strung hedgerows of Cornwall, striving to implant them upon her memory, ready for bringing out later when she was back in dreary London. After all, in the days and weeks to come, let alone the years that lay ahead, her memories might be all she had. She smiled to herself, recalling the kiss that she and Jake had shared the evening before, despite her unhappiness at the thought of the separation from the man whom she loved that loomed ahead of her. That had been a really special moment and one that she would treasure the memory of for a long time to come.

Dartmoor, when they reached it, was impressive with its vast acres of grass, interspersed with the craggy tors that Dartmoor was known for. It was deserted with not a car or another person to be seen. When Jennifer asked Jake why, he replied, 'On such a lovely day, everyone heads for the beaches, which is why I decided that today would be a good time to come. Here we are, ladies, will this do?'

Jennifer gazed through the car window. He'd parked just off the road on a wide grassy verge. As she opened the door and climbed out, the tinkling sounds of water rushing over a rock bed reached her ears and she spied the line of trees and bushes that in all probability marked out the course of a river.

'Oh, it's gorgeous,' she exclaimed. She breathed deeply. The air was crystal clear, the sky above was an azure blue, the sun blazed hotly down on them. The only sound, other than that of the running water, was the singing of birds. And as she searched the skies, she saw the skylark, hovering on high, its song an uninhibited display of sheer joy.

Jake strode to the boot of the car and retrieved the picnic hamper. Lucy had also wasted no time in freeing herself from her safety harness and she was now standing, hopping from foot to foot, at Jennifer's side.

'Come on, ' – she tugged at Jennifer's hand – 'we've been here before, Daddy and I. There's water over there. Come and see. Bring the rug and the basket, Daddy,' she called over her shoulder as she relentlessly dragged Jennifer away.

Jennifer cast a smiling, apologetic glance back at Jake and knew a happiness so complete it almost hurt when he smiled back at her, saying as he did so, with a comical little salute, 'Certainly, ma'am. Where would ma'am like me to put these things?'

His easy banter seemed to set the tone for the whole afternoon because from that moment on, the ease between the three of them seemed the most natural thing in the world. Just as Lucy had wanted, they became a family – if not in fact, then certainly in their shared emotions. The only thing that marred it for

Jennifer was the thought that in another couple of days she would be leaving – probably never to return. Firmly, so as not to spoil the time she had left with the two people she had grown to love so deeply, she pushed the dark thoughts to the back of her mind. Nothing must spoil this afternoon; nothing.

Jake spread the rug he'd thought to bring with them and then waved Jennifer down on to it.

'Cushion, ma'am?' he grinned as he threw two plump cushions down for them to lean back on before sitting down himself, right next to her. As Jennifer struggled heroically for composure, Lucy ran off a little way, to perch herself atop a strategically placed boulder. She sat her doll once more by the side of her and raised a tiny pair of child's binoculars to her eyes. 'I'll call you both if I see the ponies.'

Jennifer partially reclined backwards, her one arm bent behind her head, supporting it against the cushion, and lay, watching Lucy, her eyes half closed against the glare of the afternoon sunshine.

'Glass of wine, Jennifer?'

The richly timbred voice at her side despatched the now familiar ripple of excitement along her spine and she turned her head to look directly into a face that was absolutely still as he gazed down upon her. Only the black eyes blazed as they lazily roamed over her, the gold glints the only indication that Jake, perhaps, wasn't as cool as he sounded.

Hastily Jennifer sat up and took the glass from him. Their fingers brushed and as she watched, she saw Jake's lids lower slightly over his eyes, screening their expression from her as he had the maddening habit of doing.

'I wish you didn't have to go,' he suddenly said. 'Lucy's been like a different child since you came. She's going to miss you terribly.'

Jennifer sipped the slightly chilled white wine, regarding him over the rim of the glass as she did so. 'I'm going to miss her too.' She spoke lightly but she suspected it did nothing to conceal her anguish at Jake's words. Was that all he would regret? That she wasn't around to keep Lucy happy? It was a sobering reflection.

'Of course,' he drawled, shooting her a provocative look, 'I'll miss you too,' and with that, he grinned rakishly at her.

He'd known, was her first thought; he'd known exactly what her feelings had been then and now he was gently teasing her about it. The happiness she experienced then was indescribable. She laughed at him and watched, with no little satisfaction, as his skin paled and his breathing quickened.

Then as he held her gaze with his, he was suddenly no longer laughing. Very, very carefully, he placed his wine glass by the side of him on the grass, before taking hers from her and doing the same with that. He then lifted his hands and slid his fingers in amongst the tumbled mass of her hair, almost caressing the silken strands as he did so, before pulling her face closer to his.

'Lucy . . . .' Jennifer protested weakly.

'Lucy is too busy looking for ponies,' he murmured huskily. He bent his head and captured her parted lips, his kiss gentle and tender.

'You're so sweet, Jennifer Bell,' he said after a while.

'Mmmmm,' was all Jennifer could manage by way of

a response. She was trembling but had no chance to say anything more as Jake's lips descended again upon hers. His arms gathered her close and his kiss deepened until Jennifer could have been forgiven for believing he wanted her every bit as desperately as she wanted him. She ought to tell him the truth, she reflected vaguely. She would tell him; but not now. Not right at this moment. He was going to be angry and she wanted nothing to spoil these few rapturous hours. Tomorrow. She'd tell him tomorrow. With the decision made, she clung to him, her arms going up and round his neck, threading her fingers now in amongst the springy, dark strands of his hair. She could feel his smooth scalp beneath her finger tips. Gently, but firmly, he lowered her right down on to the cushion, moving down with her so that their bodies were side by side, straining against each other in ardent anticipation.

'Daddy, Jennifer – come quickly, come on.'

With a small sigh, Jake released her, his grin as he did so, rueful. 'I thought that was too good to last. Coming, sweetheart,' he called as, getting to his feet, he put out a hand for Jennifer to cling to and then pulled her to her feet as well.

'We'll continue this some other time. When we don't have little ears and eyes around us,' he promised, his eyes now dark with passion.

Jennifer shivered with emotion and he put an arm round her and guided her across to the rock where Lucy was bouncing up and down with exasperated impatience.

It was dark before they returned to Peacock House and then, at Lucy's bidding, it was Jennifer who put her to bed.

'Will you read me a story, please, Jennifer?' the little voice pleaded.

'Not tonight, darling. It's almost eleven o'clock. Time for all good girls to be asleep.'

'All right.' The little girl's eyelids were weighty and the thumb was already moving towards the rosebud mouth. 'Wasn't it a lovely afternoon, Jennifer?'

'Yes, Lucy, it was.'

When Jennifer got back downstairs, Jake was sitting in an armchair, obviously awaiting her.

'Well, Jennifer Bell? What now?' The expression that glittered from his eye at her told her with no shadow of a doubt, precisely what he had in mind. But Jennifer, as much as she loved him, wasn't ready for that final step, not yet. She wanted him to know the truth about her first and it was too late tonight for lengthy explanations.

'Bed, I think, don't you?' And then she bit her bottom lip in mortification as she saw what interpretation Jake had placed upon her guileless words.

He gave a shout of laughter before saying, 'I don't think you mean quite what that sounds like. Although, be assured, I'm more than ready . . . .'

'No,' Jennifer blurted out, 'I didn't.' She couldn't help but laugh even though she knew her cheeks were pink with embarrassment.

Jake got to his feet and walked across to her. He took her face between his two hands and said, 'You go to your own bed and I'll see you tomorrow. We have things to talk about and the sooner they're said the happier I'll be.' Then he bent his head and kissed her on the lips.

The next morning, Jennifer fully intended telling him exactly who she was and why she had deceived him. But, sadly, she overslept and it wasn't until the clock in her bedroom was reading eleven o'clock that she opened her eyes and realized to her dismay just how late it was. She leapt from her bed and rushed into the bathroom.

Jake and she had things to talk about; important things, he had implied. He was probably already downstairs and wondering where she was. She hadn't allowed herself to anticipate the night before what it was he wished to talk about for fear of keeping herself awake until the early hours. But now she could allow her imagination free rein and it envisaged all kinds of miraculous events; not least, hers and Jake's wedding day.

She got dressed and was running down the stairs when the front door bell rang. As she was the nearest person to it, Jennifer went to open it.

'David!' she exclaimed in some horror. David had been the very last person she expected to see.

'What on earth are you doing here?' she then went on to ask.

'Well, as I haven't heard from you – and time is passing – I thought I'd take the last few days of holiday owing to me and come down and find out what you were up to.'

'Oh, David, I'm sorry. But I've been busy – although I know that's no excuse. I should have rung you.' She hugged him warmly.

'Who are you?' The piping voice made them both turn round. It was Lucy and she was staring at David as if he had two heads at the very least. 'Why have you got your arms around her?' The blue eyes were accusing.

'Lucy,' Jennifer began, 'this is a very dear friend of mine, David. David, meet Lucy.'

But Lucy didn't respond. Instead, she glared at David and said, 'I'd better tell Daddy then.'

'Lucy, that's not necessary,' Jennifer called after her, but Lucy took no notice. She was obviously determined on fetching her father. 'Well, you'd better come in, David. You might as well meet Jake now that you're here.'

'There's been no trouble has there?' David asked. 'Only I expected you back before this.'

'No, no trouble . . . but,' she paused guiltily, 'there's something I have to tell you. Only not here, not now.' She felt guilty because the truth was that she hadn't given a thought to David in days now. She'd been so wrapped up in her inexorably growing feelings for Jake that she'd had no time for anything else. It was inexcusable. She should have made time to phone David and tell him the truth. As it was, it was too late. He was here now and about to be confronted with the man that she had chosen above him to be the recipient of her love. David was going to be so hurt.

'Here's Daddy.' It was Lucy returning, leading her father by the hand.

Jake looked every bit as displeased at seeing David as Lucy had done. His brow was dragged down into a frown.

'Jake, this is David,' Jennifer began.

Jake's gaze flicked from David's face back to hers. He'd clearly recalled her phone call to someone called

David not long after she'd first arrived at the house.

'I haven't rung him as I promised to do and he's come to see if I'm all right.'

'Why shouldn't you be?' Jake brusquely asked.

'Um . . . is it all right if we go into the lounge?'

'Certainly. Be my guests. Lucy, sweetheart,' Jake turned to his daughter, 'why don't you run off to the kitchen and ask Mrs Elliot to bring us a pot of coffee? Tell her we have an unexpected visitor.'

Jennifer eyed Jake. Where was the passionate man of yesterday? In his place was a narrow-eyed, downright hostile stranger. For Jake, she realized, was regarding David with open dislike.

Lucy, full of self-importance at being given what she saw as a very adult task, walked with great dignity from the room. Instinctively, Jennifer looked at Jake. Normally they shared their amusement at moments like this, but not this time. His gaze was coolly noncommittal as it met hers.

'So . . .' Jake began, belatedly making an effort to be polite, 'you work with . . .?'

'Kathy? No.'

Jennifer closed her eyes. Oh no. She'd forgotten to remind David that Jake and Lucy knew her only as Jennifer Bell – not Kathy Bellamy, and David had all too clearly also forgotten the content of her phone call appraising him of the fact.

Jake frowned. 'Kathy? Who's Kathy?'

David glanced at the white-faced Jennifer and grimaced ruefully. 'Sorry, love. I forgot. Have I blown things for you?'

'It's OK, David,' Jennifer said, 'I was going to confess in a moment or two anyway.' She smiled weakly at the stony-faced Jake. 'This morning actually.' Why – oh why – hadn't she told him yesterday? She'd almost done so out on the moors. It had only been her wish to avoid just such a scene as this – in front of Lucy, that had persuaded her not to. It had been a mistake. She should have told him days ago.

Jake's eyes were fixed upon Jennifer now, as were Lucy's. The little girl had come back into the room just in time to hear David's revealing words. She reached now for her father's hand. 'Who's Kathy, Daddy? This is Jennifer.'

But everyone else had ceased to exist for Jennifer. There was only her and Jake, facing each other over something that was fast turning into a bottomless chasm of misunderstanding. 'Yes, darling, that's what I thought too.' Jake's voice was grimly contemptuous.

'My name isn't Jennifer Bell – well, at least, it is . . .' Jenifer stammered haltingly. It was almost impossible for her to go on beneath the distaste that she thought she saw within Jake's eyes.

'No,' he ground out. 'It's Katherine, isn't it? Katherine Bellamy? The penny's just dropped.'

'My middle name is Jennifer.'

'And Bell is a shortened version of Bellamy. My God,' his lip curled at her, 'are you really a journalist or is that another fabrication?'

'No, I do write for the *Chronicle* under the name of Jennifer Bell. I write novels as Katherine Bellamy.'

'Yes, I know. Esther had one or two of them. So,' he drawled derisively, 'it was all very convenient. And, my goodness' – his tone now was one of biting sarcasm – 'we have something else in common. Much, much more than I had been originally anticipating.' His contemptuous glance told her that he was referring to the physical attraction that they felt for each other with his ironical words.

Jennifer stared at him, her eyes huge in her ashen face. 'D-do we?' she stammered. She hoped he wasn't going to be too indiscreet in front of David. She didn't want David to hear her news from anyone but her. But the expression upon Jake's face told her that he was way past caring who he hurt at the moment.

'We're both writers.' Jake's anger lashed her now. 'Well, I'll say this for you, Jennifer Bell or whatever your name is, you're the first woman to make such a complete fool of me. God,' he raised his gaze heavenwards, 'you even enticed me into inviting you into my home.'

'That's not fair,' Jennifer heatedly protested, 'I didn't entice you into anything.'

Jake's glance raked her with quiet deliberation. 'Oh yes you did.' The words were low and silky smooth and left Jennifer in no doubt as to what he meant. He believed she'd deliberately used the physical attraction that had been so overwhelmingly obvious between them from the very first to inveigle her way into his home and his life.

'Look, Richardson,' David interrupted, 'what's the point of tearing into Kathy – um, Jennifer . . . .'

The look of sardonic amusement that flitted across Jake's face then almost had Jennifer curling up in shame.

'Difficult, isn't it?' he murmured smoothly. 'So what shall I call you from now on? Jennifer or Katherine?'

'Please yourself,' she muttered back.

'Oh, well in that case, I'll stick to Jennifer. Better the

devil you know,' he murmured provocatively.

And even now, even in the light of the contempt that shone from Jake's face at her, Jennifer felt her stomach curl with excitement as he spoke her name. She closed her eyes again. Had she no shame?

'Here's the coffee,' sang Lucy and the three people turned as one to see Mrs Elliot carrying the tray into the room.

# Eleven

David didn't wait for coffee; he chose to leave. Jennifer was sorely tempted to go with him but she couldn't bring herself to go with Jake regarding her the way he was. She had to try and put things right between them first. Whether he'd allow her to, of course, was another matter. He was obviously feeling let down and betrayed. And why wouldn't he? She'd lied to him, stayed in his house under false pretences as far as he was concerned, made a complete fool of him as he'd already pointed out. She couldn't find it in her to blame him.

Once she'd seen David out, therefore, she returned to the lounge and two pairs of hostile and accusing eyes.

'Well, Jennifer – Katherine? What's it to be?'

'Katherine; Kathy,' she quietly said.

'Why?' Jake burst out. 'Just tell me why you've masqueraded under another name? It wasn't as if there were any need even. Why didn't you tell me when I mentioned Katherine? I gave you the perfect opening.'

'I don't know,' Kathy answered. 'I didn't set out to deceive you, Jake, I want you to know that. When I checked into the hotel, I gave the name I use for all my journalistic work – just as I always do. After all, I did come here to work. Once I'd done that it seemed to me that it would only unnecessarily complicate matters to correct it. I didn't think it was important. And I thought if people knew that I had been a friend of Esther's they wouldn't talk to me as freely as they would if they believed I was simply an impartial journalist. But I'm sorry. You're right, I should have told you once I was here in your house. But somehow, it got progressively more difficult and I thought . . . .'

'Well, go on. You thought what?' he icily demanded.

'I thought you'd ask me to go – if you knew I'd lied to you.'

'And, of course, your sordid task wasn't complete, was it? Or was that just another fabrication? That you were here to do a follow-up story on Esther? Was your real objective the dirt that everyone tried so hard to uncover at the time of Esther's death? To get one up on all the other newspapers? Was that it, Kathy?' He gave a snort of bitter laughter then. 'Well you must have succeeded beyond your wildest expectations. You've got your dirt, all right. Straight from the horse's mouth, so to speak. My God, I've told you everything. You should be able to have a field day.'

'You have my word, Jake, that nothing of what you've told me will appear in print.'

'Your word?' he scoffed. 'And what's that worth,

Katherine Bellamy? Do tell me because I no longer know.'

'Please, Jake, if I'd ever envisaged that we'd become such friends . . .'

'Friends?' Jake's smile was pure irony. 'Is that how you see us?'

'Well, yes – but also . . .' Kathy had been about to say that she also saw them as considerably more than that. Jake didn't give her the chance to finish.

'I see.'

He seemed to have calmed down somewhat and his gaze was measuring her now. Kathy took a small breath. Perhaps things were going to be all right, after all. He just needed to vent his anger upon her first. But no. His next words destroyed that hope.

'I'd like you to pack your things and go.'

They'd both forgotten about Lucy, standing there, alongside her father, taking everything in. Her tone was one of anguish as she cried, 'Daddy! Don't say that. Please.'

Jake put out a hand and touched his daughter's fair hair. 'I'm sorry, sweetheart, but it's for the best.'

Lucy tugged away from him and threw herself at Kathy. Kathy put out her arms and caught her. 'No, no,' she shouted. 'Don't go, Kathy. I want you to stay. Daddy doesn't mean it . . . .'

'I think he does, Lucy,' Kathy quietly said.

'Daddy.' Lucy ran back to her father, clutching hold of him around his leg. 'Daddy, tell her you didn't mean it.'

Jake didn't answer. His eyes blazed at Kathy, his expression one of pure intransigence. He wasn't about to back down, no matter how pitifully his daughter pleaded with him.

Resigned to the inevitable, therefore, Kathy turned and stumbled from the room. She hurried up the stairs to her bedroom and with trembling fingers did as Jake had bidden her. She packed her things. It didn't take long; she hadn't brought much with her. She'd grown used to travelling light in the course of her work; she only carried the bare essentials with her. She closed the case and then stood looking around her. There was one more thing that she wanted to do before she left this house for good. She wanted to have a look in Esther's bedroom. Mrs Elliot had told her that Jake and Esther hadn't shared a room in years, so she wouldn't be prying amongst Jake's belongings. She'd intended asking Jake's permission sometime during the course of her stay at Peacock House but somehow she'd never got round to it. It would be a pointless courtesy to ask first now, Jake would almost certainly refuse. Kathy decided to do it anyway. He'd already told her to leave. If he should discover her there, there was nothing else he could do to her – or so she thought.

She opened the door and left the room. Silently, she crossed the landing to the door of the room that she knew to be her friend's. She went in.

Deep gloom and a faint odour of mustiness met her. A glance showed heavy velvet curtains drawn across two floor-length windows. Kathy strode across and pulled one back, just enough to let some light into the room so that she could see what she was doing.

She stood and looked round her then. The room contained a massive double bed; it stood against one wall. Another wall was covered completely with a vanity unit and twin sets of wardrobes. Windows filled a third wall and upon the fourth was the door through which Kathy had entered and another door. This, upon a cursory inspection, she saw led into a luxurious, marble bathroom. It was fitted with every luxury that anyone could possibly want. She walked back into the bedroom again. Disappointingly, it told her nothing of Esther. She didn't really know what she'd been expecting, but it certainly wasn't this; a room that had been methodically and clinically stripped of every one of her friend's personal possessions. There was none of the normal paraphernalia of a woman's room, even the wardrobes stood empty, their doors slightly ajar. A single book, obviously overlooked by whoever had cleared the room, lay on a chair. Kathy walked across to it and picked it up. It was one of her own. The words 'Katherine Bellamy' seemed to mock her. She idly flicked through the pages.

So engrossed was she in her thoughts of Esther that she was oblivious to the opening of the door behind her. She heard nothing until Jake's voice drawled, 'What are you doing in here? Not still snooping, surely? Haven't you discovered enough yet for your purposes?'

Kathy swung, her expression registering her dismay at being discovered. She swung dropping the book as she did so. Jake deftly caught it and replaced it on the chair. He glanced down at it.

'Admiring your work, Ms Bellamy?'

'Not really. It wasn't one of my better efforts.'

'What are you doing here?' he asked again.

'I just wanted to have a look before I left,' she murmured. 'Perhaps discover the real Esther; the Esther that I once knew. She must still have been there – somewhere – beneath the rather superficial façade that she evidently presented to the world at large. She'd changed; dramatically and profoundly. The Esther that the local people have talked about wasn't the Esther that I recall. Something must have happened to change her . . . .'

'Yes,' muttered Jake, 'she met me and I married her.'

Kathy met his darkened gaze levelly. 'Are you saying it was your fault?'

'Yes – well – in part, at any rate. We should never have married. We weren't suited in any way. I knew that within six months of the wedding. Esther needed someone who would devote himself to her and I – well, I needed someone – ' he shrugged, his gaze suddenly fixed upon Kathy – 'more mature, I suppose. You see, Kathy, Esther never really grew up. That's why she took no interest in Lucy. She saw Lucy not as the child that she should have cared for and loved, but as a rival for my attention and everyone else's. A rival who would one day grow up and possibly be more attractive that she would be.'

'Perhaps you should have married Pauline?' she muttered bitterly. 'More your type, maybe . . .?'

Jake regarded her bleakly. 'That was a momentary aberration upon my part and one I lived to regret – as you very well know.'

'Yes,' she murmured, drily, 'I suspect Pauline lived to regret it to. After all, she lost her job because of it.'

A small smile played about Jake's lips, as he asked, 'Were you jealous of Pauline, Kathy?'

'Jealous of Pauline? Me?' she exclaimed. 'Don't be ridiculous.'

'Yes, of course, such a thing could never be. You'd have no reasons to be jealous not when you consider us just friends . . . . Although I have to say that wasn't the impression I received up on Dartmoor yesterday.' He paused. 'Or the night that I took you out to dinner. I think you felt a shade more than mere friendship then for me. . . . Perhaps, I should make some attempt to resurrect those feelings. What do you think, Kathy? Or do you use your body as well as your lips to tell lies? Is that it? Was your response simply another lie?' He was contemplating her intently as he spoke and she belatedly realized that he'd moved closer without her noticing it. His smile was deadly, in direct contrast to the heat that blazed from his eyes at her. He took another unhurried step towards her.

Kathy took a step back. 'What do you . . . ?' Her question petered out. She didn't care for the expression that filled those dark eyes, not one bit. It was threatening almost. 'What are you going to do, Jake?' she whispered tremulously.

'This.' Jake's one hand grasped her shoulder. Then her caught hold of the other with his free hand and tugged her in. She was now standing within an inch of him. Too close, she admitted.

She lifted both hands defensively between them, making a somewhat feeble attempt to ward him off. Her palms lay flat upon his chest and she felt the discernible quiver of his muscles beneath her fingertips. She tried to push him away but he wasn't going anywhere; that was only too evident. There was a quiet purposefulness about him. He grasped both of her hands and forced them down behind her, where he restrained them in just one of his. His other arm he slid about her waist. With very little effort, he had made her his prisoner; Kathy couldn't move.

'Let me go,' she said.

'No.'

'What do you want, Jake?'

'I want to disprove your theory that you and I are just good friends.' His tone was one of smooth sarcasm, as was the smile that decorated his face.

'If you would have let me finish what I was about to say downstairs . . .' she began.

'Be quiet,' he bit out roughly.

'How dare you?' Kathy made a halfhearted attempt to protest. It did her no good at all. Jake merely bent his head to hers and captured her mouth with his. His kiss wasn't a tender one, not by any means; it was ruthless and savage. It forced her lips apart, compelling her to surrender to him. He was deliberately tormenting her. But even so, Kathy couldn't suppress her tiny moan of desire as, helpless against her body's natural reflexes, she began to kiss him back. He ground his lips over hers, demandingly, and then, as suddenly as he'd reached for her, he released her. So unexpected was it, that Kathy couldn't prevent her stagger backwards and she would have fallen she was sure but for Jake shooting an arm out, grasping her and steadying her till she'd regained her balance.

'Now,' he ground the word out, 'now, you tell me that we're just friends,'

Kathy stared at him, her expression, she suspected, stricken.

'Yes, exactly as I thought. You can't. You don't regard us as friends.' His tone was brutal in its forthrightness. And as he reached for her again, Jennifer knew she could take no more. He clearly intended to heap yet more humiliation and torment upon her and she wasn't going to stand there and take it. Apart from anything else, she knew that she wouldn't be able to hide her love from him for much longer. It was a miracle he hadn't already recognized it for what it was. Add to that the fact that whatever it was Jake felt for her, it certainly wasn't love, and she knew she had to get away from him. So, before he could grasp her, she swung and ran from the room.

'Kathy,' she heard him call behind her. 'Don't go. I'm sorr—'

But Kathy didn't stop. Down the stairs she fled at breakneck speed, her suitcase and everything else forgotten in her urgent need to escape that house and Jake. He'd accused her of making a fool of him. She laughed tearfully. But, my God, he'd made an even bigger fool of her. He'd stolen everything from her: her heart, her love, her soul . . . .

She ran through the rose garden and on into the hedged garden. There were seats in there and with luck, Jake wouldn't follow her there – if he even bothered to pursue her, of course. But her haste proved her undoing. As she ran, her one foot caught in a large hole at the base of a tree as she attempted to skirt it, taking a short cut to the gateway that she knew led into the smaller enclosed garden. She went sprawling, unable to save herself, twisting her ankle beneath her as she fell. She must have blacked out momentarily because she came to to find herself lying on her back, staring up into the leafy canopy overhead. She must have struck her head as she fell because it ached abominably now. With a groan, she sat up, wincing as she did so at the pain that she felt in her foot. Her ankle seemed to swell as she stared at it. She gave another groan. Now what was she going to do? She was far enough from the house that calling probably wouldn't elicit help and she didn't know if she'd be able to stand, let alone walk. She bent forward and as she did so the glint of metal caught her eye. There was something amongst the rambling roots of the tree which was responsible for her fall. It looked like a box of some sort – pushed right inside the cavity that the root made as it sat partially revealed on the surface of the ground. Moving forward, by dint of pushing from behind with both hands and sliding over the stony ground on her bottom, Kathy managed to reach the hole. She put both hands down inside and pulled out a box. A metal box with a lid. Slowly and with intense curiosity now, she lifted the lid. Had Lucy hidden something out here? She smiled to herself. Perhaps she shouldn't be looking but she couldn't help herself. With the lid open she saw that the container held some ten or twelve navy-blue, leather-bound books. She lifted one out and opened it. A diary, and one that covered the past two years moreover. It was Esther's; she'd recognize the writing anywhere. She'd always kept a diary as a girl but Kathy wouldn't have expected her to continue the habit once she was married. Her fingers were trembling in her excitement as she realized the implications of what she'd found. This could tell her why Esther took an overdose. If her friend had been running true to form, every one of her thoughts and emotions would be recorded in this book.

'Kathy; Kathy. Where are you?'

It was Jake.

'Here, Jake. By the gate to the hedged garden.'

Jake strode round the bend in the path and headed straight for her. His eyes darkened as he saw her sitting on the ground.

'What's happened? Are you hurt?'

'Yes. Stupidly, I've fallen and wrenched my ankle. I tripped over that root . . . .'

Jake crouched down by the side of her and very, very gently began to examine the ankle and foot.

Kathy winced. As gentle as he was being, the foot was so tender that any touch, however light, was going to hurt.

'Yes, you're right. Well, that puts the lid on you leaving today at any rate.' His expression gave away nothing of his sentiments at this. He didn't seem to have noticed the box at her side.

To Kathy's astonishment, her own feeling at his statement, was only relief. She didn't want to leave him – ever.

Jake lifted his head then looked straight at her. 'It's all my fault. This whole thing. My performance in there was nothing short of disgraceful; unforgivable, in fact. I'm sorry.'

'No, it's my fault,' she argued. 'I should have been honest with you and I wasn't.'

'You did what you thought you had to,' Jake generously conceded. 'You were here to do a job, after all.' He paused, and said more slowly, 'The truth is, Kathy. . .' he paused a second time, 'I reacted so violently because . . . what have you got there?' He was staring at the box.

Kathy said nothing; she simply proffered Esther's diary. He'd soon see what it was. Jake was far too astute to need explanations. He took it from her and opened it.

'A diary. Esther's diary.' He closed it again, looking

at the dates engraved on the front cover. 'I didn't even know she kept one.' He spoke slowly as the implications of what he was holding struck him as it had Kathy. 'Why, this should tell us every. . . . '

But Kathy wasn't interested in the diaries any longer. Suddenly, it was imperative that Jake finish what he had been about to say. 'Jake,' she began, 'what were you going to say then?'

Carefully Jake replaced the diary in the box with all the others, deliberately taking his time, it seemed to an impatient Kathy. When he did finally lift his eyes to her face again, she saw the gold flecks within the dark depths that always signified intense emotion. Her breathing quickened as she waited for him to speak.

He took one of her hands in both of his and still he said nothing.

'Jake?' she breathed in anguish. 'Please, I have to know.'

'I love you,' he said with simple honesty. 'I loved you from the first moment that I saw you. It just took a while,' – he smiled tenderly at Kathy's stunned expression, because despite what she had hoped for, she hadn't really expected to hear him say such a thing – 'for me to recognize it. Never having experienced the real thing before.'

Kathy let her indrawn breath out slowly, striving for the control to speak. 'Jake,' the word came out very shakily but she managed it, 'Jake, I love you too.'

'I know you do,' he murmured. 'I realized it back there.' A sideways jerk of his head indicated the house, hidden now by the masses of bushes and trees that stood between them and it. 'What fools we've been, both of us. We very nearly lost each other.' And with that, he drew her slowly into his arms. He was by this time kneeling at her side so it was an easy matter for him to bend his head and kiss her. And that's exactly what he did. It was a kiss that shook Kathy to the core of her being. It was filled with so much love that she couldn't possibly doubt the veracity of Jake's words. She slid her arms up and around his neck, clinging onto him as if her very life depended upon it. Which, of course, now that they'd admitted their love for each other, it did.

# Twelve

'Come on, let's get you into the house and get that ankle attended to. That's priority number one; priority number two . . . .' – Jake's eyes gleamed at her – 'well, I'll tell you what that is later.'

Kathy blushed hotly. There was no mistaking his meaning. He intended making love to her.

'What is it darling?' Jake asked. He'd evidently seen the sudden shuttering of her joy, the hot flush of scarlet upon her cheek.

'Nothing,' she muttered as he hefted her up into his arms in readiness to carry her inside.

'Tell me,' Jake ordered, 'or we don't move from this spot.'

Kathy regarded him and something in the glittering of his eye told her that he'd already comprehended her inexperience.

'I'm not the experienced woman of the world that

you think me, Jake,' she said, lightly.

'I know that,' he quietly confirmed her suspicion. 'It's one of the things I love most about you. I want to be the first, my darling; the one to teach you. So, stop worrying.'

With that, she relaxed against him, sighing in her complete and utter happiness.

'Will you make Lucy and me the happiest people alive and marry me, Kathy?' he asked unexpectedly .

Kathy's head shot up from where it had been nestled in the hollow between his shoulder and throat. Her astonished gaze met a surprisingly humble one.

'M-marry you?'

'That's right. Marry me. I realize that I'm asking you to take on a ready-made family, so to speak, but . . .?'

'Yes, Jake. Yes, I'll marry you.' And so saying, she pressed her lips to his. 'Nothing would make me happier.'

Once they reached the house Jake laid her on the settee in the lounge and made sure she was completely comfortable before calling his doctor. Only when all that had been accomplished to his satisfaction did he return to the garden and collect the diaries.

'We'll examine these later,' he said. 'They're almost bound to clear up the whys and wherefores of Esther's suicide, I should think. I still can't believe that Esther was that unhappy – unhappy enough to take her own life. There had to be a reason that no one has yet discovered.'

Kathy reached out a hand to him. He took it. 'The diaries will tell us, Jake,' she said, 'I'm sure of it.

Esther always wrote everything in them. They were better than people at keeping secrets, she always said.' Kathy smiled in reminiscence. 'I'm sure they'll clear up the mystery.'

Lucy, when she was told of the forthcoming nuptuals, was ecstatic – as only a five-year-old can be.

'Kathy,' she cried, 'you're the person I most wanted to be my new mummy.'

'I'm so glad, darling,' Kathy smiled at her, her heart giving a great lurch of joy at the uncomplicated happiness shining from the little girl's face, 'because I want so much to be your new mummy.'

'We're going to be so happy, the three of us,' Lucy went on, matter-of-factly.

Jake and Kathy's eyes met across her head, their shared amusement warming Kathy as she hugged Jake's daughter to her. She was so fortunate. She'd found a man that she would always love and a child whom she couldn't love more if she were her own. Would Esther be pleased at the way things had turned out? She so wanted to think she would be.

'And who knows,' Lucy had pulled back slightly, casting her grinning father an old-fashioned look over her shoulder, 'perhaps before long, there'll be four of us.'

'That child is too advanced for her years,' Jake complained with a comical expression of resigned pride.

The doctor duly arrived and diagnosed an uncomplicated sprain, whereupon he bandaged the ankle tightly.

'Stay off it for as long as you can,' he ordered. 'Rest; that's what you need; complete rest.'

When he'd gone, Jake rejoined Kathy, after handing a protesting Lucy over to Mrs Elliot for an hour or so.

'Now,' he said, 'let's go through that diary, the last one, and hopefully, find out for once and for all, exactly what drove Esther to do what she did.'

And the final diary did indeed reveal all that they had hoped for.

It listed the names of every man who had been involved with Esther in the past two years but most importantly, it gave the name of the very last man with whom she had had an affair, Chris Williams.

Kathy gasped, as astonished as Jake was when the name was revealed.

'I can't believe it,' Kathy exclaimed. 'Chris. So Jilly was right to be suspicious.'

The affair had begin six months before Esther's death and every detail of its progress was there, written down for them to read. Kathy felt no guilt at reading the words that Esther had intended for her own eyes only. It seemed only right that she should read of the reasons for her friend's final despairing act. But neither she nor Jake had anticipated the revelations that were about to come.

They skimmed through the first pages of the book, only reading every word when they reached the time of Esther's affair with Chris Williams.

*July 20th*
*I can't wait for this evening. Thank heavens Jake is away so I can get out. Chris is so attractive. He thinks I'm beautiful. He never stops telling me so. Not like Jake who hasn't noticed me properly for*

*years. All Jake cares about are his precious shops and his books. Well, at long last I've met someone who does care about me. Chris doesn't demand that I stay at home, looking after Lucy. Chris wants me to be happy. What shall I wear tonight? It has to be something totally ravishing. After that dreary wife of his, he needs something bright; irresistible, alluring. My blue dress, I think. Yes! My blue. It highlights my eyes and does wondrous things for my skin. I want to be beautiful for Chris.*

*July 21st*
*I think I'm falling in love! For the first time ever. It makes what I felt for Jake look like a juvenile crush. . . .*

Kathy glanced sideways at Jake – to see how he was taking these disturbing revelations by the woman who had been after all still his wife at the time of her writing. Strangely, Jake didn't seem at all perturbed. His eyes flew across the words, Kathy looked back down and continued to read.

Esther had written: *He took me to The Smuggler's Arms last night. Not the place I would have chosen for our first date but as Chris said, they're discreet. Chris has some sort of deal with the manager, Robert Lowe. He wouldn't tell me what but he swears that Robert won't betray us or gossip, he has too much to lose. We had our meal in a private room upstairs. Robert himself served us. That was a turn up for the books. Robert is usually so stuck up.*

Kathy could almost hear Esther speaking. That was just the sort of phrase she loved to use.

There were many more such entries over the next months with Esther detailing the rapid progress of the love affair.

*Dec 15th*
*Chris took me to London with him. I told Jake before he left for Leeds that I was going up for a spot of Christmas shopping. He believed it! We stayed at the Ritz so Chris can't be exaggerating the extent of his dealings with Robert. He's told me what they are. Must mean he loves me as much as I love him. Or else he wouldn't have entrusted me with the details, would he? Even Jilly doesn't know. She'd probably have a fit. She's such a prude. No wonder Chris looks elsewhere for his pleasure. He's been totally honest with me. He's had other affairs over the years, the same as I have, but this time he feels differently. Just as I do. Anyway, to get back to the details of what he and Robert are doing. It's very clever, Chris loads his invoices with items that are never delivered to the hotel, the owner – with ne'er a check on whether they've actually received the items or not – pays Chris and he shares the difference between the real amount due and what they've paid with Robert. Good job he hasn't tried the same thing with Jake's lot. He'd never have got away with it. Jake checks everything and anything! Except what his wife is doing in his absences from home!!!*

'My God,' Jake muttered, 'the fools. Chris could find himself up on a fraud charge if the police got hold of this.'

And that's how the entries went on. Rapturous words

of a woman falling more and more deeply in love. Kathy was appalled. Jake seemed – unsurprised. Then suddenly, the tone of Esther's writing changed – dramatically.

*Dec 29th*
*I can't go on. I'm so unhappy. I'm not eating, sleeping. I've been to the doctor. He's given me some tranquillizers. They'll soon put me right, even help me to sleep. Chris still refuses to leave Jilly. How can he do this to me? I love him; he loves me – so he says. Nothing else should matter. It doesn't to me. I'm quite prepared to leave Jake and a luxurious lifestyle. . .why can't he be prepared to do the same? The crux of the problem apparently is that Jilly's the one with the real money and Chris says he can't afford to leave her – he owes her too much!! Owes her too much? What about what he owes me? I could finish him with just a few words dropped into the right ears – and he knows it. Then, he says he can't afford to upset Jake. He puts too much business his way . . . but if we weren't here what would it matter? He can always start the business up somewhere else. London. There are hundreds of hotels and shops there. They must import cheeses and wines. I can't understand it. I don't know what to do. But one thing I do know, I can't go on like this. I refuse to go on like this.*

Kathy could visualize her friend, pale and distraught, agonizing over what she should do. There'd been no mention of her pregnancy so far. Perhaps at this point, Esther hadn't known herself. Although, surely she must have suspected – unless she'd put any irregularity down to her worries over her love life. It would be in Esther's character to do that. She'd never been one to face up to the more unpleasant aspects of life – which was why she had found it so hard to cope with the problem of Chris Williams and his refusal to leave his wife for her.

The entries were made daily at this point and growing steadily more despairing and, as Chris obviously continued to refuse to leave Jilly, more hysterical. And that's when the threats began, the threats to ruin Chris if he didn't do what she wanted him to. Leave Jilly and run away with Esther.

Kathy, as she read, felt an increasing sense of doom. The scene was being set for tragedy – right here on these pages. They were the words and tantrums of a spoilt woman who, for once, hadn't been able to get what she wanted. Was this what had made her resort to the previously unthinkable? Suicide? Finally the evening before the one on which Esther died, the diary revealed the fact that Esther had made her decision.

> *Jan 27th*
> *I'm meeting Chris tonight. I'm going to tell him that I can't go on like this. He's got to do the right thing by me. I've been to the doctor again. He's told me I'm pregnant – with Chris's child. It must be Chris's. I know Jake and I made love once – but it was only once – it's got to be Chris's. It's given me the lever over him that I need. Jilly has never been able to give him a child and it's something he's always wanted . . . I didn't plan it. In fact, I can't understand how it happened. Must have been that time I missed taking my birth pill.*

*Perhaps it's fate taking a hand. Who knows? Thank goodness I'm off the Mogadon. I wouldn't want any risk to Chris's baby. So, I've given Chris an ultimatum. Either he tells Jilly about us or I will. When I've done that I'll tell Jake I'm leaving him and then, once I've burnt our boats, Chris will have no option but to take me away somewhere. We'll make a new life together. I'm meeting him at The Smuggler's Arms to tell him.*

*Jan 28th*
*Well, I did it. I told Chris about the baby and that I fully intend to tell both Jake and Jilly the truth. That nothing he can now say or do will stop me. He seemed stunned at first but then he came round. I knew he would, the darling. He's even agreed that we can take Lucy with us – if I want to. I'm still unsure about that. She might be better off with Jake. Sometimes Chris just needs someone else to make the decision for him Anyway, he said to leave it to him. He'd deal with it. He's promised so I've agreed not to say anything to Jake yet – not until Chris has told Jilly. I will just have to be patient. We'll go away he said. Only another twenty-four hours to wait. Chris has just rung. We're meeting at The Smuggler's Arms. He said to go to room twenty-two – the same one we've used a couple of times before – and wait for him there. He's already warned Robert. Chris has said he's got some news. He must have told Jilly! Oh, I'm so excited. By this time next week, we could be somewhere together . . . just him and me and our unborn child.*

That was the last entry that Esther had made. The following morning she was found dead, the empty wine and barbiturate bottles at her side. Kathy's sensc of doom intensified. Something was wrong with all of this. Esther hadn't been contemplating suicide; far from it, she was looking forward to a life with Chris and their, as yet, unborn child. Jake's next words echoed those fears.

'Not the writings of a woman about to kill herself and her unborn child. No mention of suicide, not one,' Jake grimly retorted. 'I would have said, after reading this, that such a thought had never entered her head. So, that leads us on to another question. Where did she get the bottle of wine from? And the barbiturates? She hadn't taken it to the hotel with her, that's for sure.'

'Chris?' Kathy whispered, her face ashen at the implications of what Jake had just said. 'Oh, my God, Jake. Did Chris give her the barbiturates and the wine?'

'It's beginning to look very much like it. Ask yourself, Kathy, what would a man be likely to do, faced with the sort of ultimatum that Esther, by her own admission, issued? Think about it. He's faced not only with the complete breakdown of a marriage that it clearly suits him to keep alive and the loss of his business – because as he quite rightly says, I am his biggest customer – but also, if Esther blabs about his dealings with Lowe, the possibility of a lengthy stretch behind bars, What would a man threatened with such consequences be capable of doing?'

'But – he couldn't force her to swallow them?' Kathy's face paled yet again. 'Jake – you don't think . . .?'

'I don't know what to think if you want the truth,

Kathy,' Jake retorted grimly. 'But I'm going to ring the police. They can read this. I think Chris Williams has some explaining to do, don't you?'

An hour later, Sergeant Toms presented himself at Peacock House and Jake handed the relevant diary over to him.

Twenty-four hours later, the sergeant returned.

'You'll be pleased to hear, Mr Richardson, that once we confronted Chris Williams with that diary he told us everything. He was almost relieved to, in fact. I think he's been a man in torment. As you suggested, he did indeed murder Mrs Richardson.' He gave a sigh. 'We're all to blame for him getting away with it till now. We accepted what our eyes were telling us far too readily. We should have delved a bit deeper. He put the barbiturates into the wine bottle and then took it along with the empty pill bottle to the hotel. He stayed with her until she'd drunk enough of the wine to become unconscious then he emptied away what little was left in the bottle, wiped both containers clean of his own prints and then made sure they were both covered with Mrs Richardson's before he left. He told Lowe as he went that he'd finished the relationship, despite Esther's threats of suicide if he did. When Lowe appeared bothered about it, Williams assured him that she wouldn't really do any such thing. Esther loved life too much. He told Lowe to just leave her alone and she'd get over it and return home to her husband. So, when she was found the next day, Lowe would think she'd simply carried that threat out. He'd never suspect Williams of being responsible. Anyway, Lowe was more disturbed at the notion of her doing it in his hotel.'

Sergeant Toms gave a satisfied little smile. 'Williams

clearly didn't know that she kept a diary . . . if it hadn't been for that, he'd have got away with it.'

'Nobody knew about the diaries, Sergeant, including me,' Jake said. 'And I certainly didn't know that she hid them in the garden. I suppose she was frightened of me finding out the details of her extra-marital affairs if ever I should come across one. No one would think of looking in amongst the roots of a tree. If Kathy hadn't fallen, they'd be there now.'

'But why did none of the staff of The Smuggler's Arms admit that she'd met someone there that night?' Kathy interrupted. 'They must have known. And, come to that, why didn't Robert Lowe tell you that Chris had been with Esther?'

'I went to see him and asked him that, Miss Bell. He said that he hadn't wished to be involved with any police enquiry – obviously due to his fraudulent dealings with Williams. He decided at the time to let sleeping dogs lie. His words, not mine. He, along with Williams, of course, are now being charged with a conspiracy to defraud. As for the remainder of the hotel staff, I don't think they did know that Mrs Richardson had met anyone that night. Or at least, nobody will admit now that they did. Frightened I'll charge them with obstructing the course of police investigations, I expect. I think if they did know then Lowe probably put the fear of God into them over it afterwards. As a consequence, everyone kept their lips tightly shut. I seem to remember him being more concerned with the hotel's reputation at the time than the fate of poor Mrs Richardson.' He smiled grimly. 'He did admit that Mr Williams and Mrs Richardson had only met there two or three times, at the most, prior to that last evening, and that it was all done with the utmost discretion. Williams would turn up to see Lowe on the pretext of business. Mrs Richardson would turn up in the bar and have a drink. All perfectly innocent. They then appeared to leave separately but, of course, in reality, would have chosen their time to make their way upstairs to whatever room Lowe had booked them into – under a false name. At the end of the evening, they left the hotel – separately and by the back entrance – to return to their respective homes. So no one was any the wiser. Not even the chambermaids. They'd just assumed that the guests who had used the room had checked out early in the morning. We'll probably never know why Mrs Richardson openly checked into a room on that last night. Perhaps she was hoping she could tempt Mr Williams into staying the night with her and, thereby, compromise him. But then, for that plan to succeed, the hotel staff would have had to know he was in there with her . . . and they won't admit to any such thing. So,' the sergeant shrugged, 'she hadn't told Williams what she'd done or so he said.'

Once the sergeant had gone, Jake took Kathy into his arms.

'I always wondered if perhaps things weren't what they seemed about Esther's suicide,' Kathy said, 'but I never, not for a moment, suspected murder.'

'No, nor me. Poor Esther,' Jake murmured. 'However unhappy we were, I would never have wished such a thing for her. Murdered by the man that she loved and trusted.'

'Wait till the papers get hold of it.' She glanced at Jake anxiously.

'Yes,' he agreed grimly. 'They'll have a field day.

Oh well, we'll just have to sit it out. They'll get bored with it in the end.'

'So Bill got what he wanted at the end of the day The story behind it all. And what a story it's turned out to be.'

'You realize that you'll be dragged into it this time, darling,' Jake said.

'I know. But as you said – we'll just have to sit it out. Providing that we can keep it all away from Lucy, I don't mind.' Kathy paused uncertainly. 'Jake . . . if you and Esther were so unhappy, why didn't you simply leave her?'

'What was the point? There was no one I wanted to be with and there was Lucy to consider.'

'Even though you believed she wasn't yours.'

'If she hadn't been it wasn't her fault, was it? Why should she be deprived of the only father she knew? Anyway, whatever I believed, I couldn't help but love her. I wouldn't have willingly given her up.'

Kathy smiled at him.

'You're really a very kind man, aren't you, in spite of the image that you present to the world at large?'

Jake raised an eyebrow at her, the familiar gold flecks making their appearance. 'And what image would that be?'

'The image of a totally ruthless, arrogant man.'

'Is that what I seem?' Jake seemed genuinely astonished.

Kathy nodded. 'It's very intimidating.'

'Hah!' Jake threw back his head and laughed. 'I didn't notice that you were intimidated for very long.'

'Well, I was, completely.'

'And are you still?' he asked, quietly now.

'No, not now that I've seen beneath the surface to the real man . . . .'

He kissed her. 'Then let's not waste any more time talking about it. Let me show you that real man. The man who loves you more than life itself, my darling.'

And with those words, he ended any further discussion between them by the very effective means of capturing her lips with his own.